For Love or Money

TIM JEAL

'When you've lived as long as I, you'll see that
every human being has his shell and that you
must take the shell into account . . . There's
no such thing as an isolated man or woman;
we're each of us made up of some cluster of
appurtenances . . . I've a great respect for
things.'

Madame Merle in *The Portrait of a Lady*.
HENRY JAMES

D1355639

ff

faber and faber

This edition first published in 2013
by Faber and Faber Ltd
Bloomsbury House, 74–77 Great Russell Street
London WC1B 3DA

Printed and bound by CPI Group (UK) Ltd, Croydon, CR0 4YY

A CIP record for this book is available from the British Library

ISBN 978-0-571-30387-8

Preface to the 2013 Edition

I wrote *For Love or Money* in about two months during my final year at Oxford when I was twenty. I knew so little about the habits of novelists that I was unaware that most would have considered this period of time inadequate even for a first draft, let alone a finished novel.

During the summer of 1965 I became convinced that I'd been working so little at Old and Middle English that I was certain to get a terrible degree. For some reason, which I now forget (probably laziness), I ruled out putting in some serious work on the English syllabus in order to avoid this debacle. Instead, I reckoned the best way to soften the inevitable blow, for myself, my parents and my favourite tutor, would be to write a publishable novel. This didn't strike me as an inevitably doomed enterprise because I'd recently won a short story competition, which, rather embarrassingly, had been sponsored by the Oxford literary society which I'd helped to found. My prize had been publication in *Town Magazine* (long-since defunct). A London literary agent, John Johnson, had read my story and told me that if I attempted anything longer he would like to see it with a view to representing me. This sliver of hope had given me the temerity to try.

I don't remember thinking about the plot and characters for very long before I started to write. Such plans as I had remained in my head. Perhaps this was why *For Love or Money* would be my only book, apart from my memoir, *Swimming with my Father* (written thirty-eight years later), that, while I was writing it, seemed to flow effortlessly from the first sentence to the last. Reading random passages from my novel all these years later, their freshness and vitality still please me.

As I started to write, my overriding objective was to finish the manuscript in a convincing way. Apart from that, I wanted to amuse and divert anyone who might one day read my book. If I could make them laugh aloud once or twice that would be a bonus; and by mixing farcical moments with sad ones, I hoped to move my readers too. I was well aware that dozens of university novels had been written in the past decade alone and that I would therefore be wise to look elsewhere for my subject-matter.

When I was thirteen, shortly after I'd left my boarding prep school, I'd gone to stay during the summer holidays with a school friend on his family's Scottish island in a decaying Victorian castle. His mother was separated from her titled husband and lived with her lover, a former army officer, who'd been one of the first men to land in France on D-Day. My friend's mother was a lot more devoted to her beloved than he to her, and when he attempted to leave the island during a storm, after a noisy argument, she threatened to kill herself. Since there were several guns in the house, her two sons and I were highly relieved when the would-be absconder failed to launch his boat on account of the vile weather and had to return to the castle. In 2004 I would give an accurate account of this incident in my memoir, but in my novel, in the 1960s, I thought it sensible not merely to change everyone's name but to transport the lovers and the boys from their Scottish island to a country house in Cornwall. In real life, both sons gave the impression of liking their mother's companion, but in the novel I provided him with a secret London love-nest (paid for with her ladyship's money), and made the elder son determined to get rid of the 'parasite' to protect his future inheritance. To achieve this he manipulates his younger brother, who, in the novel, is probably the lover's son.

I typed with two fingers on an ancient typewriter, becoming quite speedy before I'd finished, and remember parcelling up the typescript with string, not Sellotape, in my digs in Park Town and sending it to John Johnson. Two months later (the same time it had taken me to write the book) he wrote to tell me that Macmillan had accepted it, just as it was. Opening John's letter soon after my twenty-first birthday was one of the most exciting moments of my life. It was raining hard and I recall cycling to my college to find someone to tell, completely oblivious to the soaking I was getting.

This was the heyday of the gritty Northern novelists, Stan Barstow, Alan Sillitoe, and John Braine, and I ought to have anticipated that the publication of a tragi-comedy by a very young Oxford undergraduate involving a titled woman and a solidly upper-middle-class cast was unlikely to create a sensation. It didn't, but somehow it received more favourable reviews than otherwise. The best was by Francis King, who described my temporary gentleman of a lover 'as a beautifully complex and compassionate creation'. The worst . . . I always remember those, but let's not go there.

In the end my degree was no disaster - a solid second, rather than the spectacular fourth achieved by my best friend. So, really, I needn't have written my novel after all. Before it was published, I had been offered a coveted General Traineeship at the BBC, but the publication of *For Love or Money*, shortly after I began work in television, led me to undervalue the opportunity I had been given in that unique period in broadcasting history. Already, I secretly hoped that one day in the not too distant future I would be able to leave the BBC to become a full-time writer.

Tim Jeal
April 2013

Part One : 1960

❦   ❦   ❦

ONE

GEORGE put down his glass of whisky on the ledge over the wash-basin between his Arden for Men and his shaving-brush. He did so with conscious care as though the slightest noise would distract him from his immediate purpose. He turned and, going over to the bed, lifted the revolver from the patchwork bedspread; in his hand it felt small and in-effectual, little more dangerous to look at than the black telephone by the bed. Really Ruth had gone too far this time. The boys were difficult enough already without her slating him in front of them for drinking too much, if you please ... her ... drinking too much ... he flung back his arms in a dramatic gesture, almost overbalancing as he did so. Reapplying himself to his task, he spun the cham-bers and placed a bullet in two of them. Realism was essen-tial. To fill all six chambers would be too obvious ... Rasputin had needed rather more ... but for suicide ... ridiculous. Two would be adequate.

Slowly he paced back to the wash-basin watching his well-polished shoes slide over the carpet as though on ball-bear-ings. He looked at his reflection in the mirror—not bad for forty. Carefully he took another sip of whisky and replaced the glass. A face prematurely aged by tragedy? What else could be the cause of his receding hair and the all-too-evident furrows on his brow? The whisky reproached him slyly from the ledge. Well who else, living with a woman getting on for fifty and turning pious, wouldn't every now and then have a sip? And Steven ... no words of sufficient condemnation occurred to him—Steven was his mistress's elder son.

He looked at himself more carefully ... he hadn't shaved.

When they found him he'd like to be looking his best, like a child going to Sunday school, he thought sentimentally. A perfectly shaven face, a clean shirt, a well-pressed suit, just the tiny red mark in his temple. He turned round and lifted the lipstick off the chest of drawers.

To be forced to play a practical joke like this at his age ... George sighed and leaning forward let his nose press against the mirror; his breath misted the glass. Momentarily he closed his eyes and contemplated their reactions to his apparent and beautifully staged 'ending'. They'd find him lying on the bed as though asleep. The room slipped perceptibly, he hastily reopened his eyes. Then they'll be sorry. He imagined Ruth shrieking and falling down praying on her knees. Even Steven would be humbled by this room of death. He shook his head knowingly and started to lather some shaving-soap. The scene was so clearly before him that he almost wished the two bullets in the revolver weren't blanks. A little childish perhaps, but they had to be shown his value and the obvious way to do this was to show them how grief-stricken they would be at his sudden removal.

The razor slipped easily across his face from cheek bone to jaw, with a slight flick of the wrist he ran it over his chin. He felt a sharp pain just below his lower lip. A small trickle of blood mingled with the white lather. Nothing much, a little water ... but it was deeper than it looked. The blood obstinately continued. He went over to the corner cupboard and rummaged through bottles of pills and boxes of elastoplast. Funny, no cotton wool. He looked in the chest of drawers, also without success. It would have to be stopped ... it might drip on his clean shirt. Just the tiny red mark on the temple. The picture in George's mind became increasingly important as he went on searching. No, he'd have to wait until it stopped. He tucked a handkerchief into his collar like a bib to protect his shirt. Hurt a bit too. Damn stupid thing to do. Back in front of the mirror he looked at his bloodstained chin. Self-pity is most unattractive, he thought grimly. Was that really him? That half-lathered face with blood at its chin and a napkin at its neck. Ice cream and a dollop of jam. You messy man. No time for joking; his

3

mouth fell back into a straight line again. At this rate they might come up before he was ready. Shouldn't have drunk anything ... unbecoming levity. He tried thinking of more serious things; the last war, old friends, his mother, his financial dependence on Ruth, Steven's discovery of his London flat. The world's starving, the deformed, the crippled, were all given a passing thought. George sat down heavily on the bed ... perhaps, perhaps after all this little plan was just a tiny bit childish. He tried to think of the number of whiskies he'd had; remembering seemed tiring. He lay back on the bed. Better think it over ... After all, fully grown men don't play jokes. Of course his life was very tiresome ... anybody else in his position ... every now and then ... just a sip ... there were limits ... think it over ... very childish ... his head on the pillow the room became uncertain. The light bulb shone brighter than the sun. He shut his eyes.

Steven found him half an hour later.
'Yes, he was fast asleep. Covered with shaving-cream, he'd got it over his best suit, the blue one with polka-dot stripes. Lipstick on his face, too. He'd managed to cut himself ... blood all over his shirt.'
His mother sighed and philosophically helped herself to another gin. Poor dear, he really had had far too much this evening. She sighed again.

George woke up several hours later. His best suit was on the floor. Patches of dried shaving-cream spotted one sleeve and marked the back of his trousers with a displeasingly haphazard pattern. He reached out a hand to his left without raising his head. The hand groped, first slowly and then rapidly, patting the bedspread with outspread fingers. George rolled over and then stood up. Where the hell was it? He crawled about on the carpet, peering under the bed.

Was it in the cupboard? He turned out the chest of drawers. No need to panic. He felt gradually weaker as he forced his bare knees over the thick carpet. Not under the wardrobe; he crawled round the end of the bed, peering vainly at the mocking emptiness of the floor. Under the washstand, looking up, he saw it. One word, with clumsily formed letters, written on the mirror with his shaving-brush. A little dribble of dried soap hung from the bottom of each letter— NAUGHTY. George got up and looked at the chaos of his room. Very slowly, he began to undress. And no trousers too, he moaned to himself softly. He couldn't face sleeping with Ruth after his discovery. How much had the little beast told her? The question faded as he fell asleep, trouserless in his dressing-room. Ruth would be loverless tonight.

Steven perversely didn't mention 'our little secret', as he maddeningly persisted in calling it, till several days later. George had never been on very good terms with Steven, as Ruth had constantly reminded him. As a child Steven's apparent unconcern for domestic upheavals had disconcerted George more than the upheavals themselves. He had refused to call him George, but had referred to him indirectly as 'that man'. David, on the other hand ... but George was distracted before he could soothe himself with calmer thoughts of his mistress's more tractable younger son. Steven had come into his bedroom quietly. It was ten o'clock in the morning. A drab wintry light pierced the thin gap in the curtains, casting indistinct shadows on the far wall. He looked next to him; Ruth had got up.

'Didn't anybody ever...'

'You have more than once.'

'I'd rather you weren't so pert at this hour of the morning,' George answered lamely.

'Mummy was up three hours ago.'

'Good for Mummy.'

'Actually I didn't come to talk about Mummy. It's about our little secret.'

5

'I wish you wouldn't call it that.'

'Can you think of a more appealing name? "At the Point of a Gun" perhaps?'

Steven was nineteen, thin and sallow-faced with unhealthy-looking buttery-coloured hair. Or that was how George saw him.

'No?' George looked at the window as though thinking of escape.

'The reason why Mummy bought Trelawn was so that there would be no more publicity.'

'Your concern is most touching.' He rolled away from his teenage persecutor.

'Naturally I wouldn't dream of telling her about our ... it. The shock would be bad for her and there'd be rows for six months.'

'So I'm on parole. Is that it?'

'Yes.'

'You'll tell if I don't do what you want?'

'George, don't be so crude. I may have only just left school. No, George, I only ask a favour: the key of your London flat. If Mummy knew what you did with your allowance...' He clucked depreciatively.

Steven's discovery of his flat had been a disaster that could well yet become a tragedy. But as yet he had said nothing about the possibility that George might be entertaining nocturnal visitors at his mother's expense.

George turned round to face him.

'You know I could go to the Sunday papers,' he said wearily as though repeating an easily rejected formula.

'Second-rate baronesses wouldn't fetch more than five hundred pounds and your present allowance...'

Steven shut the door, but opened it a second later.

'Of course you'll fix up with Mummy about my visit to London.'

Lucky nobody was living in the flat. The thought of Steven going there was very nearly too distasteful to bear, but the thought of Ruth knowing about it was worse, far worse.

Steven stood waiting for an answer.

'I suppose you know those bullets were blanks.'

'I'm not sure what they were,' said Steven slyly.

But still this was only a secondary blackmail. This could only make him look a fool, but the flat . . .

'Yes,' he said quietly. 'I'll fix it.'

Steven shut the door.

Read all about it in the *Bumper Book for Boys*, Steven the wonder-kid hits on a wizard jape and touches his old man for a tenner. But George couldn't even manage a defensive shrug. Drinking too much really did have severe drawbacks.

TWO

CHRISTMAS came in the wake of the hols, or vacation as Steven now called it. He had just finished his first term at Oxford and had brought a friend with him. George asked the questions which he presumed were expected—what his friend was reading, what college he was at—and after that left them both alone. Mercifully for him they both spent most of the day outside shooting or talking upstairs in Steven's room. David seemed bored and out of things, irritating George with his persistent requests to play backgammon or chess. Ruth treated him intermittently with conscientious interest and neglect. George had found her interest especially irksome: inane questions about what David had done at school, receiving the expected bored answers.

'You don't have to treat him as though he's three,' said George after one of these attempts.

'But darling, I can hardly talk to him about the tin-mining industry or homosexuality.' Her tone was sincere rather than sarcastic.

'I think you might try and make him feel a bit older, that's all.'

'I know, I know only too well. But all he ever does is play with his trains and he's far too old for that. I have asked you to buy him some suitable books when you go into Truro. Yet all you get him is the Marilyn Monroe calendar ... Why, darling? It'll only remind him of Victoria and that's the last thing we want. What the eye doesn't see ...'

George winced as he looked at her expression. She stared at him with upturned face: reason murdered by the bar-

8

barians. George winced. David was nearly fifteen now. Three years ago Steven and he had stripped their little cousin Victoria behind the bamboos at the back of the house. An experience that had left her unperturbed until she told her parents. The seriousness of this affront to her young maidenhood had been so severely pointed out to her that she had quite forgotten her cousins' dumb embarrassment, as they gazed with guilty eyes on her naked eight-year-old's body. She forgot that, far from touching her, they had turned away while she dressed and had barely assisted with her undressing.

'I think enough has been said about that already,' said George.

'I don't remember you being very active at the time,' was her reply.

Dinner was the worst time for George, for then Ruth would ask Steven's friend, Robert, with mock slyness, about what her son had been up to at Oxford.

'I'm sure he's found a girl; Robert, do tell me, he has, hasn't he?' she smiled intimately, leaning forward her face between her hands. Steven cringed, not for himself, but for Robert.

'What about that little girl at Boots, Steven...' said Robert attempting to make a joke of the conversation. To his surprise Ruth took it seriously and changed the subject.

George reassured her afterwards.

'No, darling, of course he wasn't being serious, the young will have their jokes.'

'I don't like Robert. I think he may be a bad influence.'

'Seems harmless enough to me.'

Nevertheless George felt no inclination to drink and Ruth herself remained sober. One had to be thankful for small mercies, thought George sanctimoniously.

Christmas Day started well. They were drunk before lunch and sleepy by tea. At six o'clock Ruth started the drinks circulating again and George dutifully played some old 78s: *My Ideal, She's Wonderful* and of more recent vintage, *Everything's up to date in Kansas City.* This was a great success. Steven, though, suggested that his mother and George gave an exhibition dance. George, who had just drunk three whiskies too close together for stability, declined.

'All right then,' said Steven, smirking at Robert, 'this is a "ladies excuse me dance". Come on, Mumsie, get the old man on his feet.'

George looked at him with uncompromising disgust.

'Oh come on, George, darling, we'll show the younger ones.'

'Come on, George, don't spoil the fun. Play the game,' said Steven in a simpering voice.

Ruth was already on her feet. There was no going back now. George wondered how many gins she'd had. They put on *My Ideal* again and tried to fox-trot. George held her firmly, trying to avoid seeing Steven over her shoulder. The dance ended without Ruth catching her high heels in the edge of the carpet. George sat down again relieved. Everybody laughed and they all had another drink.

David had been given two new engines and a great many rails and didn't appear until dinner, so there were no tiresome requests for backgammon.

At dinner George looked across the bowl of flowers where Ruth's white hands moved in the candlelight, doling out portions of lemon meringue pie. How much had she changed? Still good-works Ruth with the Christian soul and heathen flesh. A little more skin under the chin ... after all she was forty-eight. Really remarkably few wrinkles. Of course her stomach ...

Steven was passing him a plate. George's 'thank you' came mechanically while his mind went back over the past thirteen years.

Brandy followed coffee and George sank further into his deep-wing chair, his hands folded over his stomach in those familiar surroundings of the drawing-room. The small marble clock on the mantelpiece, the mirror behind it, the flickering fire in the grate, all seemed to shimmer against the more sombre backcloth of mottled wall-paper and darkened portraits. Steven and Robert were talking softly on the sofa. David was unusually reading a book: a book George had given him for Christmas.

The evening appeared to be fading out in good-humoured mellowness. Ruth, however, decided to watch the evening Carol Service on the television. There was something about the voices of the female members of the choir which seemed to be amusing Steven and his friend. Ruth was looking at them sideways. George winked at them good-naturedly, but mistimed it. Ruth was on her feet; her face flushed, her eyes shimmering.

'Come on, old thing, only a joke,' said George level-headedly.

'In a religious service?'

David looked away. Steven's friend was looking at the carpet. George walked up to her, and held her firmly by the arm.

'Better have a rest.' He turned and said in a confidential undertone to Robert, 'Had too much.'

The three boys heard the clatter of cutlery being hurled down the passage as the choir of St. Margaret's sang on. George's voice got fainter as he retreated towards the lavatory. The noise of hammering fists testified to the firmness of the lock. Back in the drawing-room Steven walked slowly towards the television and turned up the sound, 'Ding dong merrily on high...'.

THREE

In spite of his drunkenly inept behaviour several months before, George sober rarely brooded for long over such setbacks, they were all a small price to pay for the comparative luxury he lived in.

He hadn't done a day's work since he left the Army at the end of the war and that was fifteen years ago. Ruth hadn't been precisely beautiful when he'd met her, but as the rich wife of a peer she had had other attractions for an idle young man in his mid-twenties. George was flattered and incredulous when she fell for him. His war record was good, true, but he'd never previously had any notable sexual success. Several clumsy fumbling affairs which lacked nobility and decorum, two qualities to which he had especially aspired. From cinema usherette to peeress was a step in the right direction.

His parents had done their middle-class best for him, he'd been sent to a public school, not one of the best, but nevertheless a public school. His career there had been short and uninspiring. He had not been expelled in a blaze of notoriety for stealing or perversion; his housemaster had merely suggested that the academic standards of the school did not seem suited to the steadfastness of his endeavour. It was the usual story: a succession of crammers tutored him for the Army exam but to no avail. He had just failed the first exams in the Estate Agency course, when Hitler dramatically changed the course of his life, and that of several million others, with the invasion of Poland. A few months later George was training to be an officer. His first action was in Egypt and it was there, at Sidi Barrani, that he won his M.C. It had been comparatively easy really. With six shots, one hand-grenade and five men he had captured five times that many sleeping Italians. Later on he was wounded in the back and legs at Alamein. The rest of the war was passed peacefully enough in a Yorkshire hospital and it was there that he met Ruth.

As the lady of the nearest sizeable house, she emerged once a week from an old shooting-brake to enter George's world of white corridors and sterilised floors, bringing fruit and homely small talk to the wounded.

George, who had few doubts about the war lasting much longer, had a great many more about what would happen to him when it was over. Four years ago his father had put what remained of his meagre capital into a publishing company, which he had barely lived long enough to see bankrupt. The old man had been buried in Brompton Cemetery, leaving his widow a pension and a suburban house, and his only son £2,000: a sum which, George thought lugubriously, would last him little more than a year of unemployment. And as he looked over his raised feet at the rose garden outside the ward he thought about suitable employment. Unfortunately the only jobs suitable for an officer and a gentleman demanded influence, money, or, failing that, an exemplary academic record, none of which he possessed.

The triviality of Lady Lifton's conversation and the sight of her sensible economy war-time clothes did little to alleviate his depression. She would walk from bed to bed talking to the soldiers and soon even George realised that her time spent by his bedside was as long as that paid to four others put together. Her air of complacent security and well-being irritated him, as his inattentiveness well demonstrated. She pleaded with him to take more interest in the things around him. He could hardly have pointed out that, never having enjoyed circuses, the things around him were the least likely to entertain. The man in the bed to his right was paralysed from the waist down and had lost a large part of one of his cheeks, while the only mobile member of the ward clicked past mechanically on a metal leg at half-hour intervals to the lavatory. Ruth was amazed at his rejection of the old clichés: 'fighting to recover, learning to live again'. She talked to the Sister, who assured her that his pain was no longer great. George had already been out in a wheel-chair and had twice been taken to the bathroom: on the back of the door was a Union Jack and underneath the words 'Keep Smiling'.

But as the long days passed and the sun slowly inched across the wall from the opposite beds to the end of his own counterpane, he couldn't help thinking about Ruth's home life. What was the woman doing now? Was she in the bath? On a horse? In the kitchen? Did she have dogs? What did Lord Lifton look like? How old was he? George began to look forward to those visits, visits of a person who came into his world from the security of a happier and affluent place. The kind of woman to whom he might soon be delivering groceries. What would she be like then? She probably wouldn't answer the door but would lean out from a high turret window, 'Leave them there. Cook will collect them.' And yet now she talked to him with more than compassion, even with interest. They were together as equals.

George smiled at her for the first time on her next visit and noticed too, the shape of her face, the angle of her cheek-bone, her auburn hair and dark-brown eyes. He wondered, too, what lay beneath that loose-cut coat and skirt.

Yes, he had read the book and eaten the grapes, even the bad ones. His legs were definitely better.

Perhaps when he had recovered he might come and stay with Lord Lifton and her for several weeks?

The visit never took place; before that there had been the returned pressure hand in hand, the faster breath and the half-fearful stare into each other's eyes, which said many things but one above all.

Ruth's infidelity took place a week after George's release from the nursing-home and two months before the end of the war.

The 'Lamb and Flag' was a small pub outside Ely in the flat Cambridgeshire countryside, far enough from Yorkshire to be safe. How well George had behaved. How gay and how carefree he had been. They had signed the book as Mr. and

Mrs. Byron because George had thought it funny. How the girl at the reception had blushed when Ruth laughed. A woman called Myrtle got terribly drunk that evening; her husband had been killed in Italy. She had been sitting on a stool at the corner of the bar and George had said 'That woman's had too much'. Ruth agreed, although she didn't notice. Then Myrtle had fallen off the stool and George's leg had prevented him being quick enough to stop a spaniel licking her face while she was on the floor. He had carried her to a sofa and afterwards helped her upstairs. And all this with his legs hardly healed. Ruth sat by in silent admiration. 'And so embarrassing too, the way her jersey came up at the back when you lifted her, but you were so good, George.' Goodness was a quality that Ruth admired.

The night itself was a success.

Lifton in a fit of impulsive anger had refused a divorce. George saw that there was more than a little method in his madness. Had Lifton gained the custody of his children he would have been obliged to pay for their education. A task which the size of his income rendered impossible. Steven had been nearly five at the time. They had all gone to live in a London flat and Ruth, whose private income was considerable, had engaged a cook and a nanny. George had moved in first and the others joined him two weeks later. It was then that Ruth had realised that she was pregnant; she was uncertain by whom. For the sake of the child's legitimacy, Lifton agreed to be the father in name. Besides, as Ruth argued to herself, George might not be with them for ever.

Meanwhile George did his best to leave no grounds for this uncertainty. He decided that the time had come to spend his £2,000 profitably. He bought small pieces of furniture, china, and clothes and more clothes for Ruth and Steven. She in turn provided him with silk shirts and handkerchiefs, two new suits and frequent visits to the theatre. They saw few people but remained happy. George had discovered her to be a rich woman while still at the hospital, and the discovery had increased his determination to invest his meagre patrimony with extravagant care. His recklessness after Lifton's parsimony achieved the desired effect. Ruth sold the flat and bought a house near Sloane Square. George was soon installed with all solemnity as a permanent fixture. It was in this house that David was born.

In spite of a life that exceeded George's wildest dreams of extravagance, Ruth was not happy in London. She missed the country and hated the gossip. George, who then felt insufficiently sure of his position to object, acquiesced in the move to Cornwall and Trelawn. After this Ruth rarely came to London. When George left Trelawn to go anywhere he usually did so alone.

They had been at Trelawn for twelve years now.

FOUR

DAVID went back to school two days after his fifteenth birthday on January 20th. Steven had already left for Oxford.

George was glad when the holidays were over. The last week had been particularly trying. Steven and Robert had waged an unceasing war on the rabbits, who in spite of myxomatosis were returning in ever-increasing numbers. George thought David distinctly cissy for his years and had persuaded him to come on one of these onslaughts. Quite often the rabbits were shot and only injured. This happened on this particular occasion. Steven had picked up a wounded animal by its back legs and had broken its head against the top of a fence-post with as little feeling as one might break an egg on the edge of a cup. The rabbit's front legs went on moving first quickly and then more and more slowly as though trying to escape. Only after the fifth blow when its head was no more than a mass of bloody pulp did its legs finally stop. David watched apparently unmoved and then walked off in the direction of the house. George followed his dwindling figure as he moved away slowly up the drive that rose towards Trelawn with its pseudo-gothic battlements framed by trees. The rest of them said nothing, killed a few more rabbits and went back to lunch.

George remembered that Steven had enjoyed shooting rabbits when he was as young as eleven. Then with a pen-knife he would slit open the envelope of the stomach and, holding the rabbit up, watch the still-palpitating intestines fall out and lie quivering on the ground. His interest might have been purely scientific, George felt. But David had always been revolted. An event which George remembered with especial distaste had been when David found a small bird a few summers back, caught in a patch of melted tar on the tennis court. He had tried to wash it off with paraffin but without success. Why the hell he hadn't killed it then George couldn't guess; the bird's breathing had grown difficult as the tar slowly dried on its warm body. George had put the shotgun into David's hand. At six inches there was very little left.

The day after the rabbit episode the cook elected to give them a meal that they rarely had in spite of their opportunities—rabbit pie. A dish which George secretly admitted was not one of his favourites. But David's blunt refusal to eat it seemed to be little less than sentimental.

'For heaven's sake, boy, if everybody behaved like that we'd all be vegetarians. We'd be eaten out of the country by animals.'

'I don't like rabbit pie and I won't eat it,' had been the answer.

Ruth, who had also found the pie unpleasant, further aggravated George by mentioning the forced breeding of animals.

'I suppose that goes for rabbits?' said George sarcastically.

'Anyway darling, if he doesn't like eating meat why should he? I don't see what's so funny about being vegetarian. I once knew several...'

'Well, what'd they say to him at school I'd like to know?'

Ruth really was far too soft with the boys, always had been. If she'd been a bit firmer with Steven earlier on, he wouldn't be as impossible as he was, reflected George bitterly. And as for those food cranks ... George remembered one called Rathbone, whom Ruth had known in London shortly after the war. Such a jolly fellow with his tiny sparkling eyes and boyish humour. Cold showers every morning, never had a cold in his life. His toothlessness he had sworn was nothing to do with his diet: a gum infection when young, or so he said. A fine sense of humour too when it really came to it. They'd had a corgi puppy that piddled in the brim of his hat when it fell off the hat stand in the hall.

He didn't come so often then. Probably thought flowers grew in detergent. George smiled and said:

'An uncle of mine once had a pig called Betty; fed it sugar and sweets every day. He doted on the animal. But in the end he killed her. Used to say, "I never knew how much I loved her till I tasted how good she was".'

Nobody seemed amused. George went over to the sideboard and poured himself a drink in the disapproving silence that followed. Of course it wasn't the boy's fault he was so sensitive. After all the war blunted most of us, George reflected dully. Used to be pretty sensitive myself. Cried when our pet cat was run over. Dreadful really ... you take something for granted and suddenly it isn't there any longer. His father had buried it with its collar and label on. That was the worst bit, it was so useless somehow that collar. What use was an address now, any more than the bits of cat's fish in the fridge. Still once you've seen more dead men than you're ever likely to see dead cats, you don't think like that any more.

One visit to Margate on Bank Holiday's the next best thing. All those raw meat shoulders and loose white fleshy stomachs should be enough to make the most sentimental man doubt the sanctity of human life, let alone that of the animal creation. George sat down at the table again, wise in his detachment. Perhaps he'd tell David about the cat some day. He'd already told him about the men.

That evening Ruth talked to George about David. He was so unlike Steven, much darker with a high forehead not unlike George's, and eyes the same dark brown as Ruth's.

'I don't think he's happy at school. We used to know him so well and now he's so quiet and withdrawn,' she looked at a small photograph of him taken in London holding a toy steam-roller, and then back at George. 'Perhaps he ought to have gone to a local school and come home at the week-ends. I thought he might have made a pianist but it wasn't to be.'

She sighed deeply and looked at George sitting opposite in his usual chair. He was working on a small tapestry made up of intricate if uninspired floral patterns. He had learned about needlework while he was at the Yorkshire nursing-home. Ruth smiled at him; his concentration was so endearing, he looked like he used to in the old days, slightly ridiculous in his seriousness, but that was part of his charm.

'You've got awfully big hands for those tiny stitches,' she said softly, half to herself.

Just having George opposite was a kind of security. This evening she was particularly aware of his presence; his physical solidity, those large brown shoes, his woolly socks and broad rough flannel trousers.

'I suppose he'll have to go back to school, but really George I'm not happy. He doesn't seem like other little boys now, does he?'

'I wouldn't say that, in a couple of years he'll be out of all this. I read in some book recently that the early years of puberty are always the hardest.'

He was so reassuring, she looked at him tenderly.

'George, darling, do put that stuff away, I feel awfully like bed.'

He looked up. She'd put on a new shade of lipstick and was wearing a dress he hadn't seen for several years. They say things like that make all the difference. Perhaps Lifton hadn't been a bad chooser really.

He got up, putting his work on the sofa. Arm in arm they went upstairs. 'Of course he'll be all right,' he said again.

'Sometimes, darling, I wonder why we ever quarrel,' she said, opening the bedroom door.

Two days later George was driving David between the high hedges towards Truro and his train.

David sat looking out of the window at the rain as it slanted across the glass, gathering speed as drop joined drop.

'It always seems to rain going back to school,' said David,

breaking a long silence and pulling his macintosh around him more tightly.

'Yes, it does, doesn't it. Do you remember that awful day when Mummy and I came down to see you and that fool of a waiter gave us treacle tart instead of crème caramel? It was raining then,' George ended weakly.

The rain drummed down, almost making an unbroken sound on the roof. The windscreen wipers flicked back and forth indifferently.

'Mine works better than yours,' David said gloomily as they drove into the outskirts of Truro. The clouds were getting lower.

On the platfrom George said, 'Do you want anything to read?'

'No thank you.'

'You're sure.'

'Yes.'

David appeared lost in thought. This is hopeless, thought George. The train hadn't arrived. The station smelt of disinfectant and bad milk; further up the platform, exposed to the weather, a couple of baskets of homing pigeons were getting soaked. George thought it better not to mention them.

'Nothing bothering you, is there?' George said breezily in a voice that produced the inevitable rejection.

Funny really, he might be mine and I know nothing about him. George watched the train coming in; David didn't lean out of the window in the train to wave good-bye, but found a seat and sat down.

'Good luck,' George yelled, but he couldn't have heard, wedged in his steaming compartment, between a large cherry-faced woman in Salvation Army uniform and a bony young man with watery eyes.

Driving back, George turned on the radio ... the music

sounded familiar: Schumann, he couldn't think which number ... wasn't it the one they'd heard the year she was pregnant just after the war? She had the record at home. Ruth hadn't taken him to many concerts; he hadn't been much of a music-lover, still wasn't. He left the music on though.

Strange to think of Ruth with David inside her; he'd felt quite protective, almost like a father. They'd gone for walks in the park arm in arm and he'd known what people were thinking: that's his baby in there ... another married couple.

Could have been his too, but he never felt married. He wondered why. Rather like dressing up and pretending to be a parson when you're not. Among several other parents on that platform ten minutes ago he hadn't felt even the vestiges of parenthood; nor did he feel like Ruth's husband. By putting salt on pepper you can't make everything salt. He'd joined half-way and couldn't get rid of the feeling that she'd got on to the same train five stations back. Given my circumstances nobody else would feel any different, he thought pressing his back against the driving-seat and cornering carefully. As in the parable, you can't expect much from the seed on barren ground.

He tried humming to the radio but couldn't get the tune.

It wasn't a matter of easy come easy go, it was the barren ground; that was it. Plant a grape pip and don't expect an apple-tree. Of course the arrangement hadn't been unsatisfactory; money, no strings attached, no legal ones anyway, and a comfortable life too. But it hadn't been all take either, he'd given too. Could've done something else, might be a company director by now, the best years had gone and they'd got them. If you make the game you make the rules and he thought he'd played more or less fair. There *was* the flat in London. But only once in a while ... the odd week-end. He always told Ruth he'd been seeing his mother on these occasions. Just like a great big guilty schoolboy. After all he usually did see her as well. It was clearly ridiculous to feel guilty. Any man of his age stuck to an older woman would have done the same. Really it was better for Ruth that he saw Sally every now and then. He felt better after-wards and was better to Ruth as a result. If anybody ought to complain it was Sally: she was his servicing station. Drive in for a complete wash, mental and physical. And then back home for more reliable testing and use. If Ruth paid for it, it was still for the best; she benefited indirectly.

The rain hadn't stopped. George drove on with methodi-cal care. A signpost told him he had twelve miles to go.

He hadn't gone out to find Sally, he'd met her three years ago on the Cornish Riviera Express. He'd been on his way home and she'd been going to stay with an aunt near Fal-mouth; they'd had the compartment to themselves most of the way. They'd heard each other's life stories, and she had been moved by the vision of a young army officer seduced by the lustre of an aristocratic affluent older woman. She saw chandeliers and sparkling wine in cut-glass goblets, dim rooms and full-length portraits on velvet walls. He looked at her opposite him: lively, fresh and elegant, untainted by easy luxury, and above all, young and firm, small breasts, small buttocks. The pathos of George's tale had grown as he saw what might have been.

Sally was ten years his junior and had broken off her en-gagement, having found she didn't like the man at the last moment. George asked for her address and promised that he would call when next in town. He called and that was that. Ruth seemed so much older now. Sally sympathised ... how he must have suffered in the past. He was so well dressed and so well spoken and probably had money of his own. He told her about Ruth but not the money. Honesty was not always necessary. She was old enough to look after herself he felt. Somebody who backs out of an engagement with days to spare must have some initiative. That was partly what he'd taken to, but initiative or not, he couldn't help feeling with pride that she still hoped he'd leave Ruth. Perhaps he would have done if things had been different, he thought with some bitterness. Money, the dumb god. Where did that come from? He tried to place it but couldn't ... probably Shakespeare. He had his fun every now and then but the dumb god saw that he didn't have too much.

Once, years back, he had tried to leave, but at the crucial moment the car hadn't worked. He'd made a triumphant exit, sweeping out of the house like an abdicating king, leaving Ruth and David crying. Then the damned car ... he'd thought of walking to the nearest hotel to spend the night but it was four miles away and the nearest telephone outside Trelawn was not much closer, so there was no hope of a taxi. Like most of George's unthinking actions it was doomed to failure. His clothes, everything he had was in that house. One can't take back the moves one's already played.

No, things just happened and have to be accepted. He'd gone to Yorkshire, he'd met Ruth, he'd been poor, everything had been inevitable. George felt the mantle of resignation securely on his shoulders as he turned into the drive of Trelawn.

But there was a gleam of hope. How long was it now? In three weeks he'd be seeing Sally, he imagined the flat door, the key in his hand, then telephoning her ... but now the battlemented house was clearly visible on the rise to his right. He changed down and turned off the radio. As he got nearer he couldn't help remembering that Steven had known about the flat for several months now. Luckily Sally had never decided to move in on a permanent basis. George's dislike for Steven mounted as he thought of the way he'd found out; he'd discovered several envelopes addressed to George at the same place in London and had deduced the rest. Lying to Steven was impossible. If he'd guessed about Sally he hadn't asked as yet.

George pushed open the door and entered the hall ... David would be in Devonshire by now.

FIVE

'AND if you want results you have to treat it good ... like a woman ... gently, or you won't get results.'

Sergeant Peters smiled knowledgeably as he pulled out the wireless aerial to its fullest extent with experienced fingers. Then, bending over the machine as though about to administer a kiss, he started crooning into the microphone, 'Alpha bravo, alpha bravo, alpha bravo ... tuning call...'

Round him a group of boys in battle-dress watched inattentively—one of them was David Lifton.

C.C.F. at Edgecombe School took place every Wednesday afternoon and was not a popular activity. The term was only a week old, yet David found himself listlessly slipping into the old routine as though he'd never left it.

Behind Sergeant Peters' bald head the phonetic alphabet was written on the board. It might have been the work of a lunatic: echo, charlie, golf, hotel, oscar. Fit subject for the toughest psychiatrist. David idly fiddled with a morse buzzer ... di-dah-di-da-dit-da-dit. God knows what that meant.

Outside the classroom window in the main court ten boys of assorted sizes were marching back and forth. 'About turn.' Through the closed windows the orders were sharply distinct. David thought of their hands holding the rifles ... he almost felt the cold metal ... in early February too. He shivered.

'The point of transmittin' stations is this. The world is round ... like this,' Sergeant Peters drew a wobbly circle. The chalk grated on the board. 'Now, sound waves do not go in curves, but like this.' He drew a series of unsteady tangents shooting off into outer space.

David stopped listening; in another quarter of an hour he

would be able to go back to his house, which was a good deal warmer than the classroom. The boys outside had stopped marching. Although only half past four it was already getting dark. Lights from the other side of the court showed more distinctly against the contrastingly dark brickwork.

❧

In the housemaster's drawing-room in Greville, David's house, Mr. Alfred Crofts was stubbing out a cigarette nervously.

'Really we're most terribly lucky to have got the man. A bit young perhaps, but a Cambridge Double First...' he paused to strike home the importance of this find, 'really an incredible stroke of good fortune.'

His wife continued arranging some flowers on a table in the window.

'Looks as though we're in for bit of fog tonight,' she said gloomily.

Mrs. Crofts had been in Greville some five years more than her husband. She had graduated from assistant matron to matron and had finally married the housemaster, whose wife had died of a brain tumour three years ago. The marriage had been a convenient arrangement for both of them. The housemaster gained a permanent helper to look after his two children and the matron rose to a position which she had coveted even during the late Mrs. Crofts' lifetime.

She stepped back and admired her creation from a distance. Still examining it, she started speaking.

'I shouldn't be so optimistic, I can remember any number of highly qualified house tutors who haven't worked out.'

'But Mary, he's young. The purpose of a house tutor is to get to know the boys. Who could be more suitable than a young man for that? Besides as house tutor at twenty-two if he stays at Edgecombe he'll be in an excellent position to take a house at thirty, and it's new ideas we're needing.'

'Since when have you been thinking of redundancy?'

Such a realist was Mary; he looked at her large figure

framed by the closed curtains. After years of vitamin pills and radio malt, throat-swabbing and injections, what could one expect but a practical woman? She'd always known the fakes at exam time.

'Don't be stupid dear, it's just that the house hasn't been doing so well in the Varsity awards and I thought perhaps...'

'Well look at Fowler's house, he's almost sixty and the tutor forty and they had four awards last year.'

'Ah, but in classics and history, our last tutor was a languages man. There are always more going in classics and history, and with the right man on the premises ... well we'll soon see.'

It didn't really wash and he knew it. House tutors were only responsible for a small amount of extra-curricular tuition, as well as delegating for the housemaster.

She seemed to have got, if anything, larger recently, in spite of her diet. Crofts looked at the folds of flesh that had started to appear under her chin and the downward sag of her cheeks. He also noticed that her lipstick wasn't on straight. Her mouth looked weak and formless, but her eyes behind those pink-rimmed spectacles were as hard and clear as amethysts. Still he hadn't married her for beauty. At fifty he'd been lucky to find a wife at all—he picked up a book and opened it. His wife got up.

'I'm just going to say good night to Jane.' He nodded and then started reading.

The last three years had not been kind to the house in a good many ways. Two house tutors had left and the last one had not only been thoroughly unsatisfactory but drank too. The final ugly scene had been during house prayers when he had collapsed. No, this new man was going to be a success, and if he wasn't ... nothing would be allowed to leak out.

News had also reached the headmaster of boys in his house photographing junior boys and selling the pictures in the school to seniors. Crofts' inquiries had led to nothing, although the practice on the surface appeared to have stopped. Another scandal might call his position in question. An early retirement could after all seem natural enough.

Upstairs his wife was with his daughter Jane.

'Is Jane going to be a good girl this evening? ... Of course she is. No crying tonight. Daddy's very tired this evening.'

She kissed her stepdaughter briskly on both cheeks and switched off the light.

Impressions can be pretty firmly imprinted on a child by the time it's four, she thought. She'd never approved of the way Fleda Crofts had brought up her daughter; now if *she'd* had the chance earlier, there'd be none of this whining at night. She shut the door and went downstairs to the kitchen. Once seated at the table she began to grate some cheese, turning the handle with brusque sharp movements. This new man was going to work out if she had anything to do with it. Poor Alfred, he did look so strained. The lines that ran from the side of his nose to the corners of his mouth seemed definitely more pronounced and he had developed a twitch under his right eye. But she would protect him. She had always felt sorry for him. What he had always needed was a strong personality at his side and Fleda had been such an ephemeral little person.

The lumps of cheese in the grater had already almost gone. If there was trouble this time, she at least would not shirk dealing with it thoroughly.

At the back of the same building, in another wing, David Lifton was impatiently climbing out of his rough khaki trousers. In spite of the cold he felt sticky after wearing these thick and rarely-washed clothes. There were six other beds in the dormitory but for the moment David was the only person there. When he had changed into his school suit he took a letter out of his breast pocket. It was from his mother. She told him that she was worried about him and hoped that there was nothing on his mind. Did he feel a gap of communication with her? Why hadn't he written? There really was nothing wrong? He would tell her if there was? Why hadn't he spoken to her as he used? David slowly folded the letter and replaced it in his pocket. There wasn't very much to say. He would answer each question as well as he could to reassure her.

Yet something had changed. He still loved her but recently somehow he had started to see her as though for the first time. That vague and all-enveloping rosiness contained in the word 'Mummy' had sometimes fallen away. The veil of the world of the taken-for-granted had occasionally parted and the result had been profoundly depressing. He had started to learn new things about her. It had been so easy to believe that what one saw of her was all there was to know. Anyway were these changes in him and not in her? Perhaps that was why everything seemed different. David frowned. Yet his mother's piety, her spasmodic periods of interest in him, and her violent fits of remorse for her neglect all seemed new. If she had previously concealed these flaws it was a deceitful betrayal.

David hadn't thought about George's position much. The idea of his sleeping with his mother had rarely worried him. It had all begun when he was too young to question. It became part of the taken-for-granted about Mummy, part of the impression. George became right because Mummy liked George, and because Mummy liked George, David liked George; and home was home with George and Mummy and Steven and David.

But the security of this too had begun to fade. Perhaps it had all started with the realisation that Steven and he had always seen few people, that other parents were different. During the holidays he had been looking at some books in the dusty bookcase in the hall. He'd wondered how they'd got there, having seen them for as long as he could remember. Things didn't just start after all, they were started.

Somebody bought the books years ago and then, having discarded them, pushed them into this dusty communal grave. George had been wrong when he told him that things just happened. It wasn't true. We make them happen. The pile of flies in the dust-sheeted guest-room at Trelawn hadn't always been there. They could be taken away tomorrow. Like the rabbits too—one moment alive, the next dead. That moment when Steven had gone on hitting the rabbit's head had decided him. George was wrong, George was responsible with his mother for everything that he now saw. His large brown eyes filled with tears; adolescence was certainly extremely tiresome.

Later that evening he wrote his mother the sort of letter that she expected. Why should anything be wrong? What was there in particular for him to talk to her about? School affairs probably bored her. George had always told David that a good boy who did the right things and did his work would be all right in the end.

Andrew Matthews, the new house tutor, was sitting in the bar of the 'Fox and Grapes' in the village of Edgecombe, half a mile from the school. He was alone. Since he had arrived at the school he had made no friends among his colleagues, only once having entered the common room. So far his teaching duties had not extended to private tuition in the house but apparently he was to give extra classes in classics to the brighter boys of all ages in the house, six in number.

Matthews sipped his brandy appreciatively, swilling each mouthful slowly round his tongue before swallowing it. Although it was out of his teaching syllabus, he had been exploring some medieval French Romances as night-time reading. The 'epic' love of Yvain and his fellow knight, Gawain, he found especially diverting. Chrétien was nevertheless a little harsh. Who on earth wouldn't have gone to a tournament with his boy-friend if asked, especially if the alternative was being on time for a date with a girl? And who, once there and enjoying all the fun, could possibly have remembered his previous engagement? He ran a long-fingered hand through his smooth black hair, as he started

to read of Yvain's punishment for not turning up as he had
promised:

> *Lors li monta uns torbeillous*
> *El chief si granz, que il forsane,*
> *Lors se descire...*

he clicked his tongue disapprovingly as he read on with
occasional help from the glossary. Poor old Yvain, most un-
fair. His dark eyes flicked mechanically from line to line as
he swiftly devoured the pages.

He wasn't ambitious; he'd only wanted a teaching job for
a couple of years and had been genuinely surprised when
his application for the Edgecombe job had led to an inter-
view and final acceptance. He had seen that Crofts was weak
and faded at their first meeting. Really the job should prove
amusing. Besides, as he had once read in the teacher's
manual, 'What is needed above all to be a successful
teacher is a genuine love of boys'. So conventional, he sighed
to himself, the last fling of a twenty-five-year-old adolescent
in this cruelly adult world. But the conventional aspects
were what appealed to him most in the dealings of knight
with knight in the Romances.

He looked up from his book over to where a group of
local men were playing darts. The adult male is not an
animal I admire, he reflected, stroking the base of his now
empty glass; but at public schools there were very definitely
those who made up in abundance for the shortcomings of
these louts. The more genteel pursuits of a less barbarous
age drew his eyes back to his book.

What had Henry James seen fit to call Gilbert Osmond?
'A sterile dilettante.' Ah well, there are worse callings in life,
far worse, he thought. In a quarter of an hour he had
reached the passage where Yvain received the healing oint-
ment.

Three days later David was sitting in his study, which he
shared with two other boys. He was one of the most junior

boys to be in a study, Crofts having singled him out for his undeniable aptitude in classics. Most of the junior boys lived communally in a large room known as the 'Hall'. David was sitting in a warm arm-chair looking out of the window over a vista of trees towards the playing-fields. Group of boys in football shirts and different-coloured singlets were wending their way in groups back towards their houses. Behind David, in front of the gas fire, one of his room mates, Chadwick, was making toast using a ruler with an ingenious wire attachment on the end. His mother had just sent three pots of home-made lemon curd. David wondered without much hope whether he was going to be offered some. He had, after all, parted with several tins of sardines during the past week. The grease was still evident on the fender. Chadwick started to hum tunelessly.

'Have you seen the new tutor?' Chadwick asked as he pronged another piece of bread.

'Isn't he the one with the sharp nose and scrawny-looking neck?'

'Haven't seen him. That's why I asked you, in case you hadn't guessed.'

'I'm almost sure it is.' David tried to think of something conciliatory. It was getting dangerously near the time for spreading butter and jam on the newly made toast. 'Crofts has bought a new suit,' announced Chadwick suddenly.

'Not another brown one?'

'I'm afraid so.'

'Some people never learn.'

Chadwick had been sent to the headmaster for continually chanting, 'Brown suit, brown suit', when he found himself within earshot of the housemaster and out of his line of vision. The headmaster had let him off, not having seen any Freudian undertones in the two words.

Slowly Chadwick started to gnaw his way through the three bits of toast. David went over to the gramophone and put on some Chopin waltzes.

'Do we have to have that muck?' Chadwick spluttered through half-masticated toast and lemon curd.

'Yes.'

Chadwick accepted this and started reading the evening greyhound results. He had a friend in the village who placed bets for him.

'I wonder if anybody has ever considered whether Aeneas was a homosexual,' David said thoughtfully as he opened his Vergil.

'They all were.'

Chadwick had a knack of closing conversations just when they were starting. Not even homosexuality, a topic which rarely failed with Chadwick, could make him more friendly. At least in Hall there had been people to talk to.

In two hours' time, David was due to go to Mr. Matthews for tuition on Book IV of the *Aeneid*. Before that he had to translate two hundred lines; with luck he might manage a hundred.

Andrew Matthews had not been impressed by the three pupils he had so far seen; they had been as unimaginative as they were unattractive. Perhaps the job had not after all been such a divinely given gift. But still there were three more to come today: the Honourable David Lifton, at six o'clock and Antony Chadwick at half past six. It was five to six now.

He walked over to the window and drew the curtains. His mother had made his curtains and loose covers to the measurements he had sent and in the material of his choice a chintz pattern of anemones on a white background. On the walls were several Beardsley prints and over the fireplace the *pièce de résistance* of the entire room: an oil-painting of an overflowing cornucopia—apples, bananas, pineapples, even a fish escaped from the thing to be caressed by chubby and cherubic arms. He had seen it in a London junk shop while still an undergraduate at Cambridge. Though the theme was perhaps a little bit obvious it had undeniably been an opportunity not to be missed. The picture had lived through Cambridge with him and had followed him to America, where he had done a year's postgraduate work at Yale. Of course it had been terribly expensive to ship, but as Matthews had said, 'It enabled me to show the Americans a piece of artistic vulgarity; in the hope that it will enable them to combine artistry with their undoubted talent in the vulgar.' He had even composed a couplet to be hung beneath it. A couplet regrettably unsuitable for his present occupation.

> 'Tiny prick and pudgy arm,
> Wherein lies your foetal charm?'

The series of speculative answers which had originally followed this question were not of the same order. Why did there have to be so many Bs in anatomical description? Somehow 'Baroque buttocks, button eyes' had been a staccato cadence out of keeping with the swelling curves of his cornucopian gambollers.

It had always been a grief to Andrew Matthews that God had not given him slightly softer features. His nose was thin and sharp, his cheek-bones too pronounced and his chin definitely too pointed. He looked around his room with satisfaction before sitting down behind his table. The warm glow of his gas fire nicely counteracted the colder and more ethereal light cast through his bottle-green lampshade.

He was wearing a polo-neck sweater which conveniently covered his slightly protruding Adam's apple. Occasions which demanded a tie always annoyed him.

A couple of minutes later David knocked and entered.

Andrew gave no trace of his appreciation of this new arrival, but curtly offered him a seat.

'I thought today we would talk about Book IV generally rather than getting down to translation straight away.'

David nodded assent. He had only managed to translate fifty of the required two hundred lines.

'First of all I'd like to ask you a few questions. I expect you've read the book in translation?'

David nodded again.

'Don't you think Aeneas behaves rather badly to Dido?'

'She does kill herself because he goes away.'

'So you think he should have stayed?' Andrew smiled benevolently, the perfect pedagogue.

'Yes, if ... if what happened ...'

David was blushing delightfully.

'Go on,' said Andrew encouragingly.

'If what happened in the cave is what seems to have happened.'

Andrew listened amazed. What an incredibly mature appraisal, put with such delicate reticence and charming embarrassment.

'So you think that after what happened in the cave he had pledged himself?'

'Well, he shouldn't have gone in there if he was going to leave Carthage and he must have known he would have to. I mean, he went to Carthage by mistake. He was shipwrecked.'

'What you're saying then is that he was selfish to try to find temporary consolation in a chance encounter when his destiny lay elsewhere.'

'Yes ... I mean ... I think so.'

Andrew looked at him sitting awkwardly on the edge of the sofa, and studied him more carefully ... of course it would be ridiculous to feel sentimental at this early stage, but this boy was certainly unusual. It would be impossible to try and convince him of Aeneas's higher role of founding Italy, after so deep an apprehension of the most intimate details of Aeneas's relationship with Dido. He decided to try another topic.

'You may perhaps remember that after Dido has fallen in love, Vergil represents her as a deer in flight running with the huntsman's deadly barb still in her side, doomed although she runs. Why do you think this is such a good simile?'

'Because she didn't ask to fall in love, just like animals who don't ask to be shot at.'

'I like that,' said Andrew slowly.

No mere textbook reiterations here. Fools like Crofts would label such freshness of appreciation 'scholarship material' and leave it at that. But here was what he had once been, before being choked by the cumbersome machinery of

35

academic theories and pretentions. Andrew had always been keen on the idea of successors at school: boys who would keep up the fight against oafish heartiness and enthusiasm for games that stifled sensitivity. For a moment he forgot his Adam's apple, and the angularity of his features. Now, exactly as he had wished, here was somebody seeing as he had seen, reacting as he had reacted, somebody almost re-enacting his lost years.

Andrew went on questioning and, as the half-hour drew towards a close, he became still more convinced that this was what he had come to Edgecombe for, to remember the past with all the love and self-pity of a dying man.

❧

David was getting up to go. Perhaps a word of encouragement would strike the right note.

'I think you have read this book most sensitively, yes, most sensitively,' Andrew said, smiling.

'Thank you.'

That blush again, but was there, too, a half-unconscious slyness, almost a smirk of pleasure? What guilelessness to betray feelings so natural, so evidently. On the whole Andrew was relieved to see this look. During much of the lesson David's face had worn an expression of reproachful melancholy. Those dark, dark eyes ... Andrew watched helplessly as the door shut. How could anybody think of talking to this boy of unity of minds overriding sexual considerations, or of the more athletic angle of men striving together in body and mind? He envisaged a relationship of platonic beauty, where words would be almost irrelevant in their perfect and silent understanding. He looked up at the overflowing cornucopia and the cherubs. Ah, help me, my horn of plenty, to be strong; the flesh is weak, so weak, he sighed.

Certainly the schoolmaster in love with his pupil was an obvious situation to be in, but couldn't there be a tragic pathos in this obviousness, a fundamental simplicity, in this recurring pattern? A mixture of sublime, grotesque and tragic in this unacceptable position? 'Public School Master in Squalid Case!' He spirited away this sudden apparition, this foul judgement of an alien and insensitive society. Nothing would stop him. Yes, he would take David out into the country for a cream tea in a couple of weeks. He would look at him against a backcloth of frozen branches and the countryside. Andrew had seen a convenient-looking place when he had driven to the school the week before: The Woodpecker Tea-Room at Coombe Bassett. Quiet, intimate, and remote. As it happened this was not to take place till almost a month later. Before that a 'flu epidemic of unusually vicious proportions disrupted the ordered life of Greville. Amongst its first victims was David Lifton.

Unaware of this future postponement of his plans, Andrew thought expectantly of Coombe Bassett. He went over to an arm-chair and sat down. A knock at the door heralded the arrival of Chadwick.

The following day David and Chadwick were sitting in their study. In the third arm-chair sprawled a larger boy in football clothes. His knees were caked with mud and the room had already started to smell of sweat. This boy's name was Hotson.

'If you have to be in the Second Eleven there is still no reason for you to come in here and make the place muddy and smelling like a stables,' said Chadwick slowly, stressing each word.

'This happens to be my room as well as yours.'

'Yes, and it is mine too, and if David could be bothered to express an opinion I think he'd agree that you might change before coming up here.... I sit here peacefully reading the papers and suddenly in comes bleeding Hercules ...'

David was looking at the carpet as though the grease stains had just acquired a new significance. His head had been throbbing most of the afternoon and he felt cold and shivery.

'Well then, this being a great democracy, let's put it to the vote. Those who want to see Hotson steaming like an overworked bull raise both their hands; those who do not raise their right hand.'

'Very funny, can't you even let a fellow rest before he has a shower?'

'Raise your right hand you idiot,' said Chadwick in a menacing stage whisper to David.

'Children, I'm just going,' said Hotson benignly.

David already felt too ill to take any interest in either of them.

'I wish you'd all shut up,' he said quietly.

Chadwick got up and walked out.

'Now that was foolish, very foolish,' Hotson was annoyed now for the first time. 'We'll have sour-face at it now for the next week. You have no feeling for psychology, Lifton, none at all.' He sighed with long-suffering exasperation. 'He's already cross at having a queer for a classics tutor, but now ...'

'I rather like Mr. Matthews as a matter of fact,' said David primly, adding, 'you haven't got an aspirin by any chance?'

'No.' Hotson got up and went over to the door. 'You'd better ask the matron.' He shut the door with a bang.

When he had been a child, David had suffered from severe earache. As his headache increased he began to feel the familiar stabbing pains beneath his ears.

The sanatorium in Greville was a large airy room with four beds. The matron had taken his temperature and asked him to bring his pyjamas and dressing-gown over with him.

From his bed he could see the Victorian chapel and, standing out darkly behind, the ridge of hills beyond Edgecombe. Two of the other beds were already occupied by 'flu victims. One was an older boy whom David knew only by name, and the other a junior he had known in Hall. All three felt too ill to want to talk.

The other two got better and their beds were reoccupied by new tenants, but David, though the 'flu left him after only a week, continued to suffer from earache.

At the end of ten days he was still no better. He watched yet another dawn breaking over the pinnacled chapel, having heard another night of sick-room murmurs and splutterings. The matron gave him codeine tablets, which he swallowed with hot tea served in practical blue-and-white-ringed mugs. He knew every crack and discoloration on the ceiling. Were the cracks rivers or roads? The blotches lakes or mountains? He tried to visualise it all in three dimensions.

At noon the matron came with the school doctor, Dr. Blossom. He thoroughly examined David's ears with the help of a small torch which he shone first in one ear and then in the other. He murmured to the matron and she nodded. Ten minutes later David heard that he was to go and see a London specialist the following Saturday. He was asked whether he had any relations in London with whom he could stay the night. He said that he had an uncle who might be in town that week-end. (David to avoid embarrassment, always referred to George as his uncle at school.) Could David write and find out for certain? He said he would.

There was one problem though, David didn't want to write and ask George himself. Once, he had asked George whether he would take him with him on one of his visits to London to see his ailing mother. His request had been curtly dismissed. What was he thinking of? Who would keep Mummy company and besides he didn't really want to see a sick old woman and spend a couple of uncomfortable nights in a dreary hotel. Heaven only knew ... it wasn't as if there was nothing to do at home. No, George was not the person to ask. David's mother, on the other hand, had always been vague when asked where George stayed in town. 'Oh, some hotel or other, darling.' But Steven, Steven did know. David could hardly have forgotten the time when he had burst into his room at Trelawn, less than a year ago and had announced that he had found out George's London address.

'Well, what's so marvellous in that?'

'We'll see, we'll see,' had been the perplexing answer.

'Are you going to send him post-cards?' David had asked.

'You're a bit young to understand.'

David had been hurt at the time. Of course he'd understood. Obviously George had a small flat and liked to go out to the theatre occasionally or see a film or two. What was so wrong in that? Besides, he knew his mother didn't like George going to London, so that was clearly why he hadn't told her. Anyway, as she didn't like the place, George could hardly take her too. Steven as usual had been looking for things where they hadn't been. David decided to write to Steven for the address; he would also phone his mother and find out whether George was going to London. The only person who mustn't know would be George. After all he might refuse like the time before. He could be very difficult at times. No, he'd ask his mother on the phone in an off-hand way, 'I expect George will be in London next week-end. Trelawn must be awfully lonely in term time when he's away as well.' Once he arrived outside the flat door he could hardly send him away. Perhaps he might even take him to the theatre as well. David smiled ... when he wanted he could think pretty clearly. Of course George mightn't be in London that week-end. His face fell a little. Still he hadn't been for some time and as he went about once a month there was a fair chance.

That afternoon he was allowed to telephone his mother. The matron tactfully left him alone while he did so. Everything went according to plan. Yes, poor old mumsy was going to be alone that week-end, but not to worry, George would soon be back and London always left him feeling better. Besides, it was only fair that he should see his mother every now and then. She was glad he was going to see a good specialist. Could he thank matron for her? They'd had men messing round the house re-doing the drive; but thank goodness they wouldn't have to bear all that noise for long. Otherwise nothing very exciting had happened. You know only the usual. At last David was able to ring off. His inquiry had been so well phrased that there was no chance of her mentioning it to George.

He told the matron that his uncle was going to be in London. She seemed pleased but said that he would have to write and ask for a letter of definite acceptance. One couldn't have small boys running around London all on their own, could one now? David tried not to show his dismay. Anyway he felt sure Steven could fix it. He would be able to write the letter of consent as well. Steven could be very helpful when he chose.

'Oh, by the way what is your uncle's name?'

David thought quickly.

'Esmond Flower.' It was the first name that came into his head.

'Dr. Blossom and Mr. Flower. What funny names there are about.' She laughed unsuspiciously. Silly woman, thought David. What was so splendid about her name? ... Miss Price ... very dull really.

David had just started on the letter to Steven when Andrew Matthews came into the sick room. Miss Price was on to him at once, faster than a magnetic mine, thought David.

'Oh, Mr. Matthews, you oughtn't to be in here you know,' she twittered, 'I mean you wouldn't want to be down with the 'flu.'

Andrew wasn't at all sure that he'd mind especially if he could recover in the same room as David.

'I'm not often ill, thank you,' he said coldly. 'I've come to see one of my pupils, Lifton.'

'Well, I suppose it's all right ... only don't say that I didn't warn you.'

'Not even on my death-bed, Miss Price, would I allot you the smallest particle of blame.' He nodded politely to her and turned towards David's bed. David saw him advancing towards him smiling a smile full of the sanity of the outside world. He found himself smiling back.

'I hope you're not too ill for a visitor?'

'No, sir, really I'm much better now. I feel awfully silly being ill so much longer than everybody else.'

'But why. Why should you? Keats was ill most of his life. Provided the will is strong, what can the body matter?'

Was this perhaps a little fulsome? Andrew decided not.

The boy was above the 'stiff-upper-lip' clichés which Crofts and his brethren would doubtless use. And he did look so delicately sensitive tucked up between those white sheets.

'You don't mind if I sit down on the bed, I feel so terribly tall with you so low down.'

'No, of course not, sir, why ever should I?'

Such innocence, Andrew inwardly groaned. So near and yet so far. Hastily he recalled his entirely platonic interest. The pleasures of the art gallery rather than the bed-chamber. How could so delicate a bloom be associated with rumpled sheets and bedroom smells?

David looked at him. Hotson and Chadwick had been quite wrong about him. He had come out of pure kindness. It would be impossible to make a pass in the sick room, so what other motives than sympathy could he have had for coming? He need not have come at all. That ghastly old Crofts would never have bothered, and as for his hag of a wife, she never came anywhere near any of them, ill or healthy.

'I expect you must get very bored. There isn't anything I could get you ... or anybody else?' he added hastily.

'The thrillers in the san. library aren't too bad and matron gives us fruit every other day ... so really ... it's very kind of you ...'

Matthews was delighted to see that his offer had produced that well-remembered blush. But God, what was he think-ing behind the impregnable darkness of his eyes? His eye-brows might be a palisade, his lashes sharpened stakes for all that he could hope to know. But how hopelessly inappro-priate were such coarse and military images. Andrew almost squirmed with inadequacy.

David felt so proud ... a master ... come just to see him ... and a junior too. He glowed with self-importance rather than embarrassment.

Andrew wondered whether David was in pain; he felt a deliciously sharp pang of sympathy, almost as if the pain was his.

'I wondered if you might like to come out to tea with me when you're better ... to sort of make up for all this ...' he gestured vaguely round the sick room. 'I expect an after-noon away from the school will do you good.'

'That's terribly kind of you, sir. I'd simply love to.'

He really sounded enthusiastic. Andrew purred.

'Well, good ... fine then ... let me know when you're a free man again.'

'Yes.'

Andrew rose to go.

'Thank you very much, sir. It really was most awfully good of you to come and see me.'

'Not at all ... not at all,' said Andrew breezily. All the tension had gone now and he had fixed the invitation. He hadn't quite known what the reaction would be. Now he felt like a kite in a dropping breeze, coming gently down to earth. He got up and turned as he stood in the doorway. He smiled once more and was gone.

Outside in the corridor he slapped his hands against his jacket pockets and with several light skipping steps left the building. How long would it be ... a week? Probably not long ... 'but ah methinks how slow this old moon wanes'. He hummed softly as he walked back to the main part of the house.

When he had gone David finished his letter to Steven and gave it to Miss Price to post. It ought to reach him the next day ... Tuesday ... plenty of time till Saturday.

The same evening at Trelawn, Ruth and George were sitting in the drawing-room in their usual chairs. Neither had spoken for almost an hour. The ticking of the clock on the mantelpiece was clearly audible above the crack-ling of the log fire. At last George looked up from his book.

'I forgot to ask you, who was that on the phone earlier?'

'Only David, just to tell me that he's going to a specialist in London on Saturday.'

'Why didn't you tell me at the time? You know I am interested in the boy.'

In London on Saturday? I'll say I'm interested. George pursed his lips.

'But darling, you looked so peaceful ... and I know it's stupid, but sometimes you feel so close that I sort of assume that you know everything I do.'

At a moment like this to give one this kind of rubbish. She could be absolutely maddening. He threw down his book and got up.

'And I suppose you didn't ask him where he was going to stay?'

'No darling, he didn't mention it, so I suppose the school are fixing it up. He may only go up for the day, the fast train shouldn't take more than five hours from Devonshire.'

George relaxed. She went on:

'Perhaps you could have met him in London, but I expect the school are fixing it all. Schools are like that, aren't they? ... so independent.'

'Yes, yes, of course they are.'

'So independent ... when he comes back, it's as though from another world ... there doesn't seem anything to talk about ... that's why I don't ...'

'Quite, quite, not your fault at all ... fault of the system.'

George felt he could afford to be magnanimous. He even smiled at her. Damned nasty moment but his week-end wasn't going to be ruined after all. It was Monday now, only five days to go till Saturday and Sally.

SIX

TERM at Oxford was now into the third week.

Steven was sitting at a table in his rooms. It was four o'clock in the morning. Six books of criticism lay limply open in front of him in ordered disarray. As he stared at the printed pages, isolated words stood out, jumping forward and then falling back into the distance. Six books and a text ... I'm getting pretty versatile, thought Steven without conviction. Sluggishly he continued copying chunks out of the criticism.

'The child who, like Hercules, can in his swaddling bands control the serpent and all his instruments named, is (as Hercules was to the mythographers) the Sun.'

Americans could make nonsense out of anything. Slowly the jigsaw of his essay was beginning to take shape. He looked at his watch ... only six more hours till his tutorial. At the end of his arm his pen moved very slowly.

Outside, through the tissue of mist in the quad below, he could see the first signs of a blearly and indistinct dawn. In half an hour the birds in the deanery garden would be singing.

He covered his face with his hands and rocked gently from side to side.

'Chaucer ... more sir ... force her...'

He tore the fly-leaf out of one of the books and started to compose a limerick. Afterwards he still felt bored, his eyes fixed on the lamp ... the edges of the shade crinkled slightly as he stared. Over on the windowsill an almost empty bottle of gin grinned at him ... blast the bloody stuff. Behind his eyes he felt a dull thumping ... the night stretched on in front of him endlessly.

He thought of the day before him; after his tutorial with Barnard Sarah was coming round. He smiled momentarily. Idly he wondered whether he was fond of her or whether she gratified his pride. Could it be love? After all his love needn't be conventional ... he didn't feel too bad when she wasn't there ... but because he felt no jealousy, that didn't necessarily invalidate his affection. Perhaps soon it might grow ... He went on writing ... 'Mature appreciation ... thought patterns ... underlying symbolism ... vivid contrasts of light and dark, good and evil...' The words were at last beginning to race in the familiar way, pouring into the well-cut channels of pseudo-scholarship. *'Gefallen sind die Blätter ... blät ... blät ... blät.'* Pure unadulterated cock, he sighed to himself contentedly. His watch showed half past seven.

A soft knock sounded behind him and he turned to see the peasant features of his scout Morgan appearing in the growing gap between door and wall.

'You're up early, sir ... or should I say late? ... Ha ... ha...' his laughter petered out in a tubercular fit of coughing.

'Wicked out this morning, sir. Fog's something awful.'

'Yes.'

'Shall I be making your bed, sir?'

That laugh again. Steven turned round and looked at him in the face.

'All right then, sir. I'll be leaving you.'

Tiptoeing like a robber in a silent film he made for the door. Steven reapplied himself to his task, desperately he looked for a concluding quote. In the end he wrote his own. He got up and went to lie down on the sofa, his legs felt unsteady. Just like poor old fuddled George, he thought. Sarah ... in three hours she'd be sitting in that chair. Somehow it seemed less important now that the essay was over.

He must have been dozing; it was five minutes till his

46

tutorial. His eyes followed the carpet patterns, first the blue shapes and then the pink. Each time he tried it became more complex. Eventually he shut his eyes, then jerking into action he heaved himself to his feet. He picked his gown from the floor; bat-like he flapped his arms until it fell into place.

His tutor Barnard had his rooms on the other side of the same quad. He reached the staircase, climbed a flight, knocked and entered. Barnard was perched like an eagle on the edge of a low contemporary table. For once Steven didn't find him funny.

'You look tired, Lifton.'

You look old, thought Steven. Barnard was about forty-five, a few whisps of still brown hair stuck out on his otherwise bald head, as though inexpertly glued on. Behind thick glasses his eyes sparkled actively as if in soda water.

'I didn't sleep well.'

'Well, what lucubrations have you brought to me this morning; a work of sound scholarship I trust.'

His laugh was surprisingly high for such a large man. He unfolded his legs and stood up.

'Sit down, sit down,' he said, flapping his arms up and down. Steven's eyes rested on his large hands. The noise of traffic came up from the street below. Barnard's room faced the quad and backed on to the street.

'Can we have it then?'

Steven started to read; his tongue felt thick and swollen. The words seemed large and lump-like, isolated boulders in a wilderness of irrelevant matter. They wouldn't cohere. The sentences were longer than usual. He sensed Barnard crossing and uncrossing his legs opposite.

'Why not try it a bit faster?' he broke in at last.

Steven complied. The sentences started to flow, punctuation ceased to matter. Somewhere in his mouth a hinge seemed to have broken: sentence ran into sentence in a whirling, racing stream of nonsense. Must finish the essay.

47

'I'll read it,' said a distant Barnard.

Barnard read. Steven felt his eyes closing. How heavy his lids had become. Barnard read on and on. Steven tried to think out of which critic each passage came. Soon he gave up the struggle. His eyes shut and Barnard read on alone.

'Well, let's try and talk about it,' Barnard was saying.

Steven woke up and tried. Barnard was getting cross. He perched on the edge of the table again. A watery sun marked the carpet in patches. Barnard's large black shoes glistened like newly melted tar. Why couldn't he stop for a few minutes? Steven eyed him warily, there were unpleasant vestiges of a smile wrinkling the edges of his tutor's mouth. The corners slowly lifted. Steven waited for the coming bombardment without hope.

'One point you don't seem to have raised in your essay is why Chaucer doesn't let us know whether the dreamer knows of the dark knight's loss earlier. I mean are we to suppose he had a reason? Or does he mean us to think the dreamer is an imbecile? Come now, this is a cardinal point. Why does this really matter?'

Barnard, still on the low table, craned forward eagerly, ready to pounce. Suddenly Steven didn't care. A middle-aged man sat in front of him awkwardly balanced on a low table. A man old enough to know better.

In the street outside shoppers were streaming in and out of Woolworths. A gob of phlegm lay in the gutter. Sparrows were twittering in the eaves. Barnard was getting restive. Have to answer soon. Answer what? What about the gob of phlegm? The sun was slowly edging across the carpet towards Steven's chair. The clear beams cut channels sharply in the stale air of the room. Steven's mouth opened.

'I don't think it really matters.'

Barnard was on his feet, his arms were working up and down frantically. No eagle now, more like an ineffectual butterfly.

'Point of scholarship ... academic interest ... cardinal importance ... fundamental significance.' Steven heard the phrases from a distance. Suddenly Barnard opened fire. A broadside ... Steven sank without a trace.

'Get out!'

❦

Back in the quad Barnard was in his place again; a small brown beetle under the radiator. Viciously Steven stabbed his feet down on the paving stones. At the bottom of his staircase he halted. In his pigeon-hole was a letter with a Devon postmark. He opened David's letter and started to read, still standing there. For the first time in the day he smiled a long and satisfied smile. Barnard might have been in Africa now. Oh, George; this, George, is it. Now I can see my way.

He climbed the stairs, took off his clothes and clambered naked into bed. Gratefully he closed his eyes and went to sleep. Behind the thick blue curtains the sun was breaking up the last of the morning mist.

At noon he heard a soft voice calling his name from the doorway of his bedroom. His face climbed over the edge of the sheets.

'Wassat.'

'Me.'

Sarah was slim and small. Almost everything about her was small, her waist, her voice, her pleasantly formed lips, even her shoes. Only her grey eyes were large.

'Oh, it's you.'

She came over and sat on the bed.

'How was Barnard?'

'Hell, absolute offal.'

'You don't look upset,' she slipped a hand through his hair.

'No, I had a letter.'

'Yes.' She had tensed. Steven smirked.

'From a very dear friend.'

'If you're trying to make me feel jealous...'

'I'm doing pretty well ... quite, quite ... in fact I was going to tell you that this very dear friend is sorting out all my problems.'

'Come on, out with it then,' she jabbed at the bedclothes playfully. Clearly it wasn't another girl.

'Ah, my vision in black, this is a dark, dark secret.'

She pursed her mouth into a small circle and turned away from him.

'Well, I won't bother you then.'

'Good.'

Her back turned, he leapt out of bed and into a dressing-gown. Next he ripped back the curtains.

'The sun, the sun,' he yelled, 'Miss Twiss, Miss Twiss, the sun is shining, God has sent good news, and I'm in love.'

She looked at him dubiously after this outburst.

'So?'

'I've told you.'

Under his dressing-gown he slipped on a pair of pants and then some trousers. Running over to the wash-basin he seized a towel and draped it round him.

'Can Caesar tell a lie?' he boomed.

'Steven, you've only just got up...'

'Sarah, my empress, don't I look just a teeny weeny bit like Nero?' a hunched be-toga'd Steven croaked, preening himself over by the mirror.

'You're quite fundamentally, absolutely impossible,' she went over to him and slipped her arms round his neck. He let the towel fall.

'Sarah,' no trace of humour was in his voice now, '... Sarah, sometimes I could almost marry you.'

He watched her expression change. Apparently the forbidden word had been spoken. A small tear appeared at the corner of each eye, soon they were streaming down her cheeks. She broke away from him and sank down on the bed. With her head between her knees, her whole body shook in spasms. Steven went on dressing. He leered at his reflection in the mirror ... on balance it had been a pretty satisfactory morning. He turned to her. Then walking over to the bed he put his arms round her.

'To make a joke of that...' she managed to say.

'But don't you understand? I'm serious, Sarah ... perhaps it might be a good idea.'

'You've only known me four months,' she looked up, mascara was streaked down her cheeks in dirty lines. Steven turned away.

'There's nothing exceptional in that.'

Of course it had only been four months but he felt as sure of her as he could be. She at least—the Lord only knew why—loved him more than anybody he had ever known. Granted there had already been scenes, her clinging, him angry and indifferent. But marriages aren't dropped from the sky, they are arranged and then worked out. There was one occasion he remembered especially well ... it had been early morning and he'd been leaving her. She'd been crying like now ... her face blotchy, no make-up on her eyes. He'd tried to feel involved, held her in his arms but it had made no difference. He hadn't been really there ... he didn't understand her tears, hadn't wanted to. She said when he asked her that he wouldn't understand, so he didn't ask again. He tried to break away and get to the door, but she had got out of bed, her nightdress up round her waist and ran after him begging him not to go. He could still hear her feet on the boards, she didn't seem to run one foot at a time but in a falling rush until she'd found him again. She had been cold and shivering but he still strode out of the house leaving her shivering in the hall of her digs. Yes, she loved him all right. Most of the time she put up a bantering façade of resistance but in the end ... Yet her dependence didn't revolt him, it was genuinely touching. Steven didn't want a domineering wife. Being dominated had never appealed to him. Rather ordinary really, he thought complacently.

But why this morning of all mornings? He held Sarah closer ... one day was as good as another. No, Steven had his reasons. He thought of the letter. If it didn't work out ... if all his suspicions were wrong? But somehow he didn't think they were. Marriage really mightn't be a bad idea.

Sarah had stopped crying. Poor girl, he buried his head in

the warm hollow between neck and shoulder. Poor Sarah, innocence in this world is sadly out of place.

'Will you take me out to lunch?' She seemed eager.

'Naturally. I've never been engaged before, not even tentatively. We'd better go somewhere good.'

She managed a smile, and then walked over to the mirror to make up again.

'I look such a mess...' She turned round to look at him, 'You weren't joking were you, Steven? You did mean it ... didn't you ...'

There was a slight tremor in her voice.

'I've never been more serious.'

She turned round again, Steven looked at her back. Sarah Twiss from neat suburban Pinner, with a mind and body as neat and trim as a Pinner garden hedge. Inwardly he felt more pity than he had thought himself capable of. So small, so young ... and so necessary. In fact Sarah was in her last year at Oxford and was two years older than him.

After lunch, Steven went round to see his friend Robert (the same Robert who had come to Trelawn the previous Christmas). Robert lived in another quad of the same college. The buildings had just been refaced, the stone was a clean warm ochre, the lawn a pleasing green. As he entered Robert's staircase Steven gazed across the quad with an air of possession.

Robert was lying on the floor in front of his electric fire. Several books lay close to him but his head was resting on the carpet.

'I've come to talk to you,' Steven said, bending down next to him.

'Must have dropped off ... what time is it?'

'Look, Robert, I need advice. You're about the only friend I've got here. I want to put a case to you.'

Robert nodded; Steven looked unusually serious.

'Has Barnard been bugging you?'

'No, no, far more serious than that.'

'Christ, you haven't got Sarah pregnant?'

'Keep calm, Robert, it's about home.'

'Yes ... ?'

Steven watched Robert sitting up; he was interested.

'Robert ...' Steven paused; then, choosing his words carefully, he went on slowly. 'If your mother lived with a man who you thought was spending too much of her money on another woman, what would you do?'

Steven watched him carefully. 'Think hard, I know these arguments pretty well. I just want to see if there are any loopholes.'

Robert did not answer at once.

'I suppose it depends how much use the man is.'

'Exactly. The man used to be very useful; he helped run the house and above all he kept Mummy happy. She is a difficult woman, as you know: thoroughly unstable ... can be as sharp as a razor and the next moment as sentimental as a schoolgirl. But now I'm not so sure that George is playing his part. You saw them together last Christmas. I'm not certain, but I think George is losing control.'

'Well, hadn't you better be quite certain?'

'No, I'm quite sure enough. This is really a minor point. I found the address of his London flat six months ago and I've discovered the approximate rent from a landlord in the same street. If George is not doing his job properly, then his pay must be reduced.'

'Why don't you warn him?'

'I have, but I don't want him to feel that I might play any final cards. I don't want to commit myself. He might panic and get rid of the flat, and without the flat I won't be able to get rid of him when it's convenient.'

'How are you going to reduce his spending?'

'I'm afraid I can't without losing my weapon.'

'Then you'll have to get rid of him sooner than you want.'

'Robert, there are times when I think you're worth your scholarship.'

Robert shrugged. Steven went on.

'As it's ultimately David's and my money that he's spending, I feel that more interests are at stake than his and

Mummy's. I don't know how much she's got left, but I do know—although it may be momentarily inconvenient—that when the ideal occasion for removing George comes ... it should be taken. The time may not be perfect, but the chance has come.'

Somebody was playing the trumpet in a room on the other side of the quad, the same tune again and again. The sun was getting lower and the room was almost in darkness. It was already beginning to feel colder. Robert turned on the other bar of the electric fire.

'So you're going to take it?' Robert asked unnecessarily. Steven ignored the question.

'Mummy thinks a lot of the money he gets goes on keeping his old mother but I'm almost sure she keeps herself. Every year that passes he's spending at least £3,000 of our money. If I told Mummy about the flat ... had George followed and that sort of thing ... found out about his infidelity for certain ... do you suppose she'd be grateful to me?'

'Of course not.'

'Precisely, what the eye doesn't see etcetera ... she'd curse the day that I'd been born for ruining the protective cocoon of her ignorance.'

'But she wouldn't cut you off?'

'I'm the elder son. She can act impulsively; she might change the will in favour of David; she wouldn't cut me off.'

'Can't you make it look as though it wasn't you ... some coincidence? I could see him with her and tell you.'

'No good, I'd have to tell her when it came to revealing. There's only one person who can finish him without ruining me and that's David.'

'So you say: "Be a good boy, David, here's the address, hop along to London, and you'll find George in bed with a lovely bit." Highly intelligent.'

'I had a letter this morning...' Steven's eyes were shimmering in the steadily darkening room. The college bells were ringing for early evensong. 'The letter was from David...'

Steven explained to Robert. When he had done so he went on:

'He leaves the specialist at five-thirty on this coming Saturday and should be at the flat by six. It's perfect, he can't miss them.'

'And if he does?'

'It will be a pity. But the flat will still be there. I'll have to think again.'

'But even if all goes well, your mother will still know that you gave him the address.'

'But don't you see, he'll have asked me for it. My action will appear to be unpremeditated ... I happen to know the address at which George usually stays when in town.... David asked me, so I saw nothing wrong in giving it him. After all I needn't have even been suspicious. She can't mind-read.'

'What about David then?'

'Oh, he'll be all right; bit of a shock for him, but George always said that he ought to grow up a bit. It'll so obviously be a freak of chance that Mummy won't suspect him of malice. She knows he hasn't got it in him anyway. Besides there's another aspect, once the thing's discovered the exact causes are likely to be blurred. She won't feel in the mood for detective work.'

'Are you absolutely sure that George has got another woman?'

'No proof ... but I don't think you can seriously tell me that he'd spend £1,500 for a week-end-a-month flat if he didn't "entertain". I've stayed in the place ... extremely well-appointed. Of course he'd removed any possible evidence before I got there.'

'I'm surprised you didn't find out about the woman earlier ... knowing the address.'

'Robert, I've already explained, I wouldn't be able to use the information without harming myself.'

Robert got up from the floor and went over to the cupboard. Steven heard the clattering of tea cups.

'Thought we might have some tea.' Steven nodded. 'The only thing that occurs to me ...' Robert mumbled, his head

in the cupboard, still searching for another cup. 'Thing is ...
what happens to your mother when he's gone? Big ships
take little ones with them.'

'She'll cling to anything left which isn't firmly out of her
grasp.'

Robert looked up sharply.

'So you'll have to get out before Saturday in fact, which
leaves David ...'

'I'm afraid you couldn't have put it better than I myself.'

'That's where Sarah ...' Robert wasn't smiling. 'May I be
the first to offer you my congratulations.'

'You really do astonish me, you can be so perceptive.'

'So David's left with Mum and you marry Sarah and try
to grab your share before anything else happens.'

'That's right ... of course as you seem to have guessed I
became engaged this morning. An engagement is I think
firm enough for the moment. Mummy wouldn't want me to
break the girl's little heart.'

'Christ, if I astonish you, you leave me bleeding speech-
less. You're really going to live your life to the letter of the
theory.'

'Life comes first and theories after and because of life's
problems.'

'Well, thank you very much indeed, Mr. Machiavelli, for
coming along and talking on "Woman's Hour" ... I'm sure
that a lot of ...'

'Not now, Robert.'

'In nomine filio ...'

'Robert, I came for advice ...'

'I'm afraid my advice won't be much use; you know what
I feel about Sarah.'

'Try and give the "she's too good for you" stuff a miss ...
try and be unbiased.'

'Unlike you, I can't separate mind from body ...'

'Don't be so bloody self-righteous. Anyway it should be
reason from emotion ... a rather different proposition I
think you'll agree. I wasn't proposing indifference to sleeping with an ape.'

'I've listened well, Steven; I've answered your questions

and asked others. Don't ask for more, you can't expect me to agree with you as well. If there are any loopholes you will have seen them. In theory I can see no flaws. But Steven in weeks, in months, years ... this room and my answers now ... you'll pay.'

'Banquo, I didn't come for philosophy; I came for logical replies. You have given me both and I'm grateful.'

Steven got up. 'I really am grateful, Robert,' he added, smiling. A second later and the door had closed behind him.

Going down the stairs he grinned; silly of him, he should have remembered that Robert had been in love with Sarah ... still might be for all that. He ought to know ... Robert was, after all, his best friend. One day he'd find out what made him really tick. It was difficult to imagine Robert in love, he was always so sensible. Yes, one day he'd ask him about himself ... might be quite amusing.

Outside in the quad again, Steven wished he'd brought a coat. He buttoned his jacket to the top and turned up the collar.

Back in his rooms he sat down at the table. With one arm he swept all the remains of last night's industry on to the floor. He then pulled a writing-pad out of the drawer and began on the first of the two letters. He complimented David on his idea ... of course it would be nice to see George, he would probably be quite pleased to see him when he arrived. Absolutely right, there was no point in letting him know beforehand. Probably he *would* say no. The letter was easy really. The second was easier still. He decided to type it. He dated it for the following day and put the address of George's flat at the top.

DEAR MATRON,

Of course I should be only too pleased to see my nephew on Saturday, and he is most welcome to stay the night. I have not seen him for almost a year and expect he has changed considerably.

I well remember his having earache when younger; in fact I was constantly asking my sister to take him to a specialist then.

Please give David my love and tell him I look forward to seeing him.

That ought to convince them of Esmond Flower's undoubted existence. He put the letter in an envelope and typed the address. He then enclosed it in a larger envelope, with a note of explanation to a friend in London, who was to post the enclosed letter from there on arrival. The matron was probably a fool, but no risks could be taken even with the postmark.

The whole process had taken barely half an hour. Steven looked at the envelopes on the table ... the end of an era, all for the price of two stamps and a train ticket. He felt specially pleased with the one to the matron. The intimations of previous knowledge of the child's health and the tone of kindly concern, struck exactly the right note.

The end of an era ... he sat back in his chair and closed his eyes...

> 'Everything's up to date in Kansas City,
> 'Cos it's gone about as far as it can go.'

He hummed gently. Perhaps it was sad in a way ... he had a drink and started to get into the mood. And yet how could any of it be taken seriously? The pre-war clothes and hats, the ancient wirelesses and telephones, the daring of women smoking cigarettes? Of course all that had been new once. But now it was just so funny, it all tied into the drawing-room comedy of his home life where nobody worked and where every action was part of a game to stave off boredom. And when all else fails let's try the drunkenness game. My God, they'd been so empty that they'd have rows for no reason at all except to change the pitch of the tedium. And then drawing-room comedy, with its animal card-games and backgammon, descended to music-hall farce, with flying cutlery and hiding in the lavatory. Only an existence like his mother's and George's could combine unthinking whimsy with meaningless indignity. They weren't stupid, they'd just lost the art of applying what wisdom they once had. There was nothing really for them to apply it to. Now the only glimmers of practicality came out in the parables of George's clichés. Perhaps his mother's growing interest in religion had some point. At least if God loves you, you don't have to hear his answers to protestations of fidelity.

Steven got up and went over to the sofa. Where are the fighter pilots now? Fat and sexless ... just like George. And the Spitfires and the Hurricanes, those brave little toys, are as useless as air-rifles. Those were the days when red pillar boxes and suet pud meant 'Land of Hope and Glory' and the red buses were symbols of democracy. Old films he'd seen showed armoured cars rolling through Parliament Square and uniforms in every street. All the brave and young were fighting ... his father Lifton had been unfit ... 'Young wives with elder husbands, there's time to have some fun ... how about voluntary get-togethers with our fighting boys ... visit a hospital or two and take your choice. Have a soldier for your love ... everybody who isn't fighting is past it, or getting white feathers with the post.' To be bitter about the period that raised up George would be stupid ... now the bomb-sites have given way to council flats and the only people who strut around in uniforms with medals, disabled servicemen.

We ought to hold open house for the North-country charabancs. Drawing-room comedy isn't over yet, and music hall has a new lease of life at devil-may-care Trelawn. Back to the thirties and early forties ... see George VI in a bathing-suit with shoulder straps singing at a seaside boys' club. Princess Elizabeth is still doing her bit in the uniform of the W.A.T.S. But put away the picture books and it's all a bit clearer ... George the idle opportunist with bed sores and his mother, a woman who had seen nothing in trousers except Lifton for ten years and felt that it was time for a last fling. And now did she still see him as the handsome young officer? Steven winced, she probably did if one could judge by the way she sometimes looked at him. But those gay years are coming to an end ... 'Ending of an Era', read all about it.

He got up off the sofa and snatched up the letters. Slowly he walked down the stairs, across the quad, out of the archway into the street and then towards the post office. The last post for Devonshire didn't leave till ten. As he heard the letters hit the bottom of the box he suddenly wondered whether he did really dislike George. If he'd been in his shoes and offered an opportunity like that ... but speculation always complicates. He dismissed the issue and with it the possibility that George possessed a grain of humanity.

If people behave like caricatures, like caricatures they must be treated. Steven had made up his mind.

Later that evening he left a note for Sarah in the college messenger box: 'Meant what I said.'

The following day David got Steven's letter. He read it eagerly; really Steven could be most helpful when he chose.

SEVEN

I t was Saturday at Trelawn.

George was carrying a small suitcase out to the car. Ruth watched him from the dining-room window. He had looked so nice at breakfast in his dark-grey suit, and the olive-green tie against a white shirt had been just right somehow. It really was awfully sentimental but he hadn't changed much since she first met him ... after all those years too ... just like yesterday. His teeth were no longer perfect but after all her's hadn't been either even at thirty-seven ... that couldn't have been ten years ago ... but it was. How strange time is ... Through the window she could see him coming back towards the house, his shoes crunching on the gravel. So this was to be good-bye till Monday. Ruth hated these moments, it was so silly too ... there he'd be again on Monday afternoon ... but the house was terribly lonely without him. She turned absently towards the breakfast table and put the top on the marmalade. She could hear him in the hall. She was watching the door as it started to open. George smiled at her. He seemed to hate these moments too, he always tried to be so cheerful, but she knew.

'Well, I suppose I must be on my way now, Ruth darling.'

'I suppose so ... but George I do hate it when you're away.'

'Don't much care for it myself ... still, really must go and see the old mother, haven't seen her for nearly a month and I don't think she's got much longer to go.' He looked at the carpet. She might last another ten years.

'Do you know we'll have known each other fifteen years next Thursday?'

'No ... no ... it doesn't seem that long does it?'

'I was thinking that too just a moment ago ... funny that you ...'

George started to move his weight from one foot to the other. Once she got on to this sort of track she could go on for hours.

'I really must be getting along now. You know what the traffic's like these days.' He slapped his pockets and made as if to turn towards the door. She probably *didn't* know what it was like, he reflected, not having been further than Exeter in the past ten years.

'Mm,' she said vaguely, as though she had not heard what he had said. 'You know sometimes when you're away I wake up in the night ... turn over and expect to ...'

He came up to her and put his arms round her neck. Her dress was too low cut. If you're not the right shape it's no good pretending.

'It isn't for long; anybody might think we'd only known each other a week.'

'But darling, that's just how it feels. They say there's a one for everybody ... I've just been lucky ...'

George felt that this would be a good note to part on. He broke away and blew her a kiss from the door. These scenes of young love were quite intolerable. If she could only see herself doing it. He shut the hall door behind him.

Soon the gates of Trelawn were behind him and he was driving through the countryside towards the London road.

Ruth had gone back to the window and watched till the car disappeared round a bend in the drive behind a group of beech-trees. If he ever left me I think I'd die, she thought mournfully. There would be the children to comfort her, but it wouldn't be the same.

Perhaps, to take her mind off things, she'd tell cook to go home to the village for the week-end. She'd prepare him something special for dinner on Monday evening when he got back. But there'd be no point in starting till tomorrow. She glanced round the room ... what was that mark on the ceiling? There was a little black spot just above the window ... was it a slug ... or could it be a piece of fallen plaster? Some of the ceilings did need doing rather. She moved a chair over to the window and got up on to it ... yes, it was a small hole, there were also one or two cracks not so noticeable from the ground. It was time the place was redecorated. She'd have the banisters revarnished too and perhaps a new stair-carpet. She got down from the chair and shook her head. One gets so used to everything that one tends not to notice. She took out her handkerchief from her sleeve and dusted along the windowsill. Mrs. Hocking and her daughter really weren't very efficient cleaners. But what could one expect ... they didn't live in.

Ruth had made a point of having as few people as possible coming in to do domestic chores. Just George, herself and the children had been the idea. Of course the cook came in every day but she went back to the village after supper.

What else could she have redone? It was time they had some new loose covers in the drawing-room. She wouldn't tell George but would keep it all a surprise. It would be horrid with all those strange men tramping all over the place but it would be worth it.

She heard a knock at the door ... the post. The only letter was for her. She looked at it with a frightful feeling of constriction in her chest. It was from her bank. She had had a letter at the end of the previous year telling her that she would soon have to sell more shares to clear her overdraft. How many years had she been living outside her income? A number of shares had gone already. The letter was worse than she had expected. Unless she cut down her annual spending, at the present rate there would be less than ten thousand left at the end of three years. The roof had been done at the end of the year before and that had cost £5,000. The house was far too big, a lot of the rooms weren't used ... but it was home. The place where they had all been so happy. Perhaps she really would have to sell it ... but not yet. Besides if she did that George would know the situation and he must never know ... he would blame himself so terribly ... and the thought of him having to take a job was too awful. She looked at the letter for several minutes and then tore it into tiny fragments. Carefully she dropped them into a tea cup.

Suddenly she knew what she would do; she'd go for a walk and try and forget about it for the moment. It was such a lovely day for the time of year ... even so she'd wrap up well ... find her wellingtons ... and go for a good long walk like a little girl, and come back red-cheeked and hungry to eat something nice and hot for lunch. Perhaps she'd have a little drink as well. She felt better already. Bank managers are always such pessimists. It must be living with all that money round them all day.

Perhaps if George and she had nothing they would buy a tiny cottage somewhere. She'd always rather liked Wales. They would be able to live on almost nothing, make their own bread, and perhaps George could make money with his needlework. After all money isn't everything. Perhaps if she had been poorer they would all have been just as happy ... even happier. She smiled to herself and went to find the wellingtons. And on Sunday she would go to the village church for evensong. They had candles for evensong. Sometimes I feel I don't deserve to be so happy, God, she said quietly to herself, as she slipped on a pair of socks over her stockings before putting on the boots.

At half past twelve George had reached a small village between Okehampton and Exeter and was feeling hungry. He saw a quiet-looking pub and stopped. He'd have a drink and perhaps they would have some home-made *pâté*. As it happened they didn't. On the bar a lighthouse made of pennies was nearing completion. He turned out his pockets and added another five. These sort of things tended to make service better. He asked for a pint of beer ... hadn't had beer for ages ... when was it now? He couldn't remember.

How nice it was to be able to sit back and eat lunch by oneself in a charming wayside inn, alone with one's thoughts. He ordered steak, tomatoes and new potatoes. After that he would have apple pie with crumbling home-made pastry. Of course he would be able to pour on the cream himself. The steak was beautifully tender and the knife pleasantly sharp. He sank it effortlessly into the meat, slightly charred on the outside but succulently tender within.

After he had thanked the pub keeper he asked him if there was a bridle-path near by. He thought he might find time for a short stroll before starting again. Days like this in late February were so rare. Yes, there was a path. Through his jacket he could just feel the warmth of the sun. On the naked twigs of the hedgerow drops of water shone in the sunshine, tiny crystal circles of glass. Underfoot the ground still felt hard with the frost and his shoes crunched satisfy-ingly at each step. He reached the top of a rise and looked down into the valley he had left; the ribbed furrows of a ploughed field, the clear grey of a slate roof, and the smudges of dried bracken all merged in this perfect scene. Not long till spring, he thought. Already the sap would be rising.

He patted his stomach and let out a slight burp of content-ment, then he started back towards the car. He breathed in deeply and almost felt the sharp freshness of the air cleans-ing his lungs. He turned and took one last look at the view.

In five hours he would be in London. Back in the car he started the engine and let off the handbrake. He felt like a song: it would help to pass the journey. Fifteen years since he had met Ruth, he really did not feel that much older to-day. In an uncertain baritone. he began singing *She's Won-derful*. His thoughts drifted along the ribbon of road before him towards London and Sally. He put his foot down a little harder and went on singing. Spring was definitely coming.

Miss Price had packed David a sandwich lunch and as nobody else had been available Mrs. Crofts had driven him into Exeter to catch his train.

'And when you get there, no nonsense, we don't want you

late for your appointment ... I know what boys are ... dilly dally ... just get straight into a taxi when you arrive. Mr. Crofts has given you the money. And after your appointment go straight over to your uncle's flat. I might even ring up this evening.'

Her hands looked alarmingly large, clutching the wheel. She was wearing a thick green sweater with the sleeves pulled up slightly, revealing strong-looking arms covered with a soft dark fuzz. David felt suddenly sorry for Crofts.

Once in the train he opened a thriller out of the sick-room library. He thought of Hotson and Chadwick, they'd just be coming out of maths. A wonderful sense of freedom welled up inside him as the sun streamed through the compartment window. George was bound to be pleased to see him. Besides he had been ill and illness is an excuse for anything. They'd almost certainly see a play or at least a film. He settled down to his book again.

'Miss White, for God's sake, there are six mistakes in this letter. Is anything the matter?... I'm only asking for you to concentrate a bit harder.'

Sally looked over the table at her employer. These young directors really were a pain. Now Mr. Thorn had been so much more considerate and of course so much older and more experienced in matters of human understanding.

'No, nothing's the matter.'

The dictating went on. Through the slats of the venetian blind the bars of sunlight were getting weaker. The noise of a calculating-machine in the next-door office was just audible.

'...with regard to the large poster for ... we should be most...'

Sally hammered on viciously. She'd just had an extremely annoying telephone call from her sister. Slipping a disk today of all days. Unless somebody could be found to look after her baby niece, she would have to give up her evening with George. Everything had been such hell recently and he was so sympathetic. He would be able to sort everything out. She'd simply have to find a baby-sitter. In the next letter she put in ten mistakes.

'I'm afraid I don't feel very well ... rather a headache...'

Five minutes later Sally was in the tube on her way home.

Dr. Everett had made even less efforts with his waiting-room than most doctors or specialists. David was sitting apprehensively on a tubular chair under a huge abstract collage. His eyes strayed over the spotless parquet floor. There were a few old copies of *Queen* on a low modern table. He was getting up to take one to read when the door opened.

'David Lifton? ... will you come this way, please?'

The weary and polite formula. How many times a day...

Dr. Everett was sitting behind a large marble-topped desk. A desk calendar with red lettering and numerals showed the date: 'February 27th, 1960. He picked up an expensive-looking fountain-pen and, poising it over a small note pad, said,

'Now when did the trouble start...?'

A quarter of an hour later he was writing out prescriptions and letters to the matron and the school doctor.

'If it doesn't go, you'll have to come back, but I hope that won't be necessary.' He handed David a small bottle of red pills. 'In the meantime if the pain continues take one of these every three hours.'

David had nearly reached the door of the doctor's flat when he remembered his coat in the waiting-room. An elderly man was sitting hunched on a chair in the corner; a woman, evidently his wife, was sitting next to him holding his hand. David apologetically walked across the room to where his coat was resting on the back of a chair. His shoes sounded loudly on the parquet floor. The man didn't look up. Perhaps he was wishing his wife wasn't there. David noticed that her other hand was shaking. How terrible that personal suffering had to be shared by others. How frightening that a single freak of chance—like a car turning out of a side-street—could change so many lives; how much simpler it would be if everyone's lives were not so closely interwoven, if single threads didn't affect the whole fabric. He sighed.

In the street it was almost dark. Dr. Everett's flat was in a large block of flats on the north side of the park between Notting Hill Gate and Marble Arch. There didn't seem much point in catching a bus down Church Street to George's flat, which was just off High Street, Kensington. He might as well walk through the park. If it was shut, the railings weren't very high. After all there was no point in hurrying, George was just as likely to be there at seven as at six.

Sally put down the telephone ... Thank God for that ... she poured herself another gin. The baby-sitter ought to be round in ten minutes. She had known that fate couldn't be so unkind to her ... Of course it was an awful thing to have happened to poor Marjory ... on any other day she would have gone straight over without a word ... disks can be so painful ... but today really was such a special one. She wondered if he'd like her new dress, especially the lace frills ... didn't they have those sort of things when he was younger?

In front of the mirror she started to make-up with care. Perhaps the green eye shadow was a little too ... a bit common ... but George always said that the young could get away with anything. She had also got a new shade of lipstick ... shocking something ... she'd got rid of the container, it had 'Sixpence off' written on it ... she pursed her lips together, then smiled at her reflection. The black dress with the lace made her look even younger than usual. Her short blonde hair just framed her face as far as the bottom of her ears. She took off her ring and her heavy bracelet. No jewellery would be needed. George had told her that her youth made other adornment unnecessary. He'd put it better than that; it had been in front of a jewellers. Since then she had

68

never shown any interest in that sort of shop window when walking with him. With the help of a piece of cotton wool she took off a little of the eye shadow ... more youthful and chaste ... better.

The door bell rang ... 'Yes, I've left some jam ... and there are the aspirins just in case ... he's newly changed ... I shouldn't think you ought to have any trouble.'

She went into the hall and phoned for a taxi. She'd only be a quarter of an hour late. Perhaps ten minutes if the man hurried.

The door bell rang and she ran down the stairs. She gave the driver the address and asked him to hurry. Soon they were speeding past South Kensington Underground Station. He was doing so well she'd give him a really good tip.

David jumped down from the railings. He was alone in the empty park. He could make out in the darkness the outline of the children's swings and slide. When he'd been ten or twelve he'd come to London for three weeks with his mother. They had come to be near his dying grandmother ... there had never been times for walks, but once or twice they had come to Kensington Gardens. He'd wanted to try the slide then but his mother had said that the other children looked too rough. He started to walk in the direction of the playground. More railings; he swiftly put a foot into the slot above the lock on the gate and pulled the other foot on to the top between the spikes. Another second and he'd be down. He jumped, there was a sharp ripping noise ... hell ... oh well, it didn't matter ... only a small tear in his trousers ... He climbed to the top of the slide and let himself go. It didn't seem as long as it had looked from a distance ... might try the miniature roundabout. Holding on to one of the bars, he started running round ... ought to be fast enough now; he leapt on and lay back on top of the the thing. He held on with his feet hitched under the rim of the round metal boss in the centre. He let his head hang down right over the edge. As his hair streamed, he looked out behind him, the lights of the park merged in an unbroken line as he spun around. The trees, too, lost their individuality, their irregularities destroyed; the lights of the houses on the edge of the park had tails like shooting-stars. It would be much easier to see people like that ... perhaps that was why George and his mother drank. Hello, good-bye ... hello, good-bye ... no need to say anything else. No features ... only blurred faces ... no knowledge of secrets ...

Alone, the only person in two square miles of empty park, David felt suddenly a god. What could any of those millions of people sitting down to supper behind those flashing lights mean to him? What possible effect could they have on him. This must be what it's like to be God ... just passing lights. How could fate or destiny care about the acts of these faceless millions? The roundabout was slowing down and as it did so the magic disappeared. Far above him David could make out the red and green lights of an aeroplane. He got off and walked a few giddy steps, one of the multitude again. How many counties could the pilot see? He thought of Crofts and Chadwick, Miss Price and Andrew Matthews. All of them confined in Devonshire and here was he answerable to nobody by himself in London. He felt the same irresponsible freedom that he had experienced on the train. What did it matter when he got back to the flat? He wouldn't go back now ... he'd buy himself a dinner first. He had a pound and his ticket back to Devonshire was already paid. He climbed out of the playground and started in the direction of The Round Pond and Gloucester Road. And on those far-off walks with his mother he had watched other children sailing boats, but it had been the kites that had really fascinated him. One afternoon he had sat near a quiet white-haired man, sitting in a deck-chair holding a large reel of twine in his lap. Occasionally he had let the reel spin out more twine. The kite was almost invisible, a tiny speck of red in all that blue, far above the week-end crowded park. The picture was still frozen for him like a lantern slide. Why did somebody so old still fly kites? David had looked at him more carefully as though the answer might be externally apparent. But his face gave away nothing. Perhaps it was the freedom of the kite ... its escape from all the people below. Perhaps his thoughts passed up the string like bits of paper until he was almost there too. At last David had dared ask a question,

'How far away is it?'

'Over Hyde Park Corner I expect.' The old man smiled a secret personal smile.

'If you cut the string would it go on for ever?'

'I'm afraid it would fall straight down.'

Freedom ... David walked on thinking ... it was all very complicated. He was beginning to feel cold and hungry ... there had to be people.

He found a snack bar near the main gates of the Gardens. Egg, bacon and chips seemed a good idea. After supper he'd look for the flat.

Sally stood outside the door of George's flat, she pulled a small mirror out of her bag and looked at herself ... not bad; she patted a few stray wisps of hair back into place and rang the bell.

'I thought I wasn't going to be able to come...' She let her bag slip and ran into his arms.

George disengaged himself and shut the door.

'Well, you don't appear to be at all surprised ... aren't you going to ask me why I very nearly couldn't come?' She knew he liked it when she pretended to be cross. She slipped out of her coat and let it fall to the floor in a blue heap.

'I always like you when you pout ... anyway you're here and that's all that matters.'

As George led her into the sitting-room Sally forgot about her sister and her grief which she had thought of telling him about. She walked across the room in front of him; before she reached a chair he patted her tight little bottom. She sat down and gave him her most virginal smile. George looked at her ... the little minx ... but she seemed better-looking than he could remember her ever having been. There really was no denying it, he was a lucky devil ... why, there'd be any number of younger fellows who would give their eyes for a girl like her. Across the room she was sitting primly in her arm-chair with her legs neatly tucked up under her.

Most of the decorations in the flat had been chosen by Sally. The dove-grey carpet, the lilac curtains, the unostentatiously patterned wall-paper, even the pictures—mostly flower prints—had been chosen by her. Sally looked around her; perhaps it was a little effeminate for a man's flat but it must be a pleasant change for him after home. She had visions of smoke-filled rooms and open fires, hunting horns on the walls. It might all be very grand in a large house with the huge portraits and everything but it couldn't be homely really. How could that woman who had spent all her life in draughty mansions know anything about the snug intimacy of the ideal-flat interior? Of course, she'd had to be very careful to see that everything was tasteful. Men like George expected that. Not that she would have wanted a musical cocktail cabinet or anything like that, not really anyway. And he'd shown how much he had liked it all by buying a lovely set of white-painted imitation Chippendale chairs, with blue velvet seats to go with the carpet.

Sally's father had been crushed to death in a munitions factory during the war. She had been eight at the time. Her mother had gone out charring to support her family, so Sally had been left with her two brothers all day during school holidays. They had ignored her with ruthless efficiency. This, combined with the assault of a slightly older boy at school, had left her frightened of men in her own age group. True, her broken engagement had been to a man of twenty-five, but that was probably why it hadn't worked out. And although one didn't like to be at all snobby, he hadn't been a real gentleman. Dick had been so inexperienced and fumbling somehow ... no assurance or poise. He'd never known about the right sort of restaurants. One time they'd driven around Soho for almost an hour before he'd seen one he liked the look of, and then it had been little better than a snack bar. It had been so embarrassing too when they'd gone to smart places; he never knew how much to tip and once asked for Nuits St. Georges thinking it was a white wine. George had laughed like anything when she told him that. But it wasn't really funny, it was a bit sad. And Dick was so mean too ... he wasn't doing badly but he still lived with his mother ... at his age living with one's mother ... All because he was mean ... On one of the few occasions that they ate at a really exotic club, she'd ordered smoked salmon with scampi to follow and after that *coq au vin* ... said he wasn't hungry and didn't want more than ravioli and coffee.

George had gone out into the kitchen to fix up dinner ... he hadn't told her what they were having ... it was to be a surprise ... He really was sweet ... it was probably because he had seen so much of life. He had fought in the war and been wounded. He'd lived with a demanding older woman and looked after her and understood her children. Only a man of real nobility would have sacrificed his life for a woman like that ... why, he'd told her that pity alone kept him with her now. How he must have suffered; if only she could make up for it. Only a gentleman ... But she wasn't ashamed of her humble origins. She'd had to work, mind you, and there was nothing to be ashamed of in that. One had to work if one was going to be able to leave all that behind ... not every little tuppeny-halfpenny shop girl would have been able to attract a man like that ... be able to talk to him. But she'd done pretty well for herself ... personal secretary to the managing director of a large department store meant a good deal of responsibility. Breaking with her mother had been difficult. That was the trouble with definite ties ... one long sacrifice.

She finished the remains of her drink and went over to the drinks cupboard to get herself another.

No, the present arrangement was the best possible ... limited domesticity without any rows. If you see somebody twelve times a year you're not likely to quarrel. She did see others every now and then ... and yet George was very close ... almost a father ... rather a naughty one.

73

George was standing in the doorway.

'Dinner is served, madam,' he bowed obsequiously. Then, coming over to her chair, he ran a hand over her knees and under her skirt. He reached the smooth warm skin above the stocking tops and playfully tweaked the suspender so that it slapped back on to her leg.

'Naughty ... butler's don't do that sort of thing I'm sure,' she pouted. But there was nothing crude about the way he did things like that. He made it seem so natural.

George withdrew his hand quickly ... no point in getting worked up with dinner still to be eaten. The advantage of having it twelve times a year was that when the time came, my God one wanted it. If she knew what it was like to feel such lust ... if only ... He watched her walk over to the door in front of him; couldn't be enlarged prostate at his age but the thought of that silky skin moving, rubbing under her skirt made his breath catch and produced an almost painful ache in his chest.

Ridiculous ... almost middle-aged and with a none-too-hidden paunch. Not much to do with love ... too blunted he thought sadly ... they say it isn't the same without love, must be the most enormous confidence trick ever to keep adolescents off it. In an hour he would be in the warm hutch of lust and forgetfulness ... or something pretty near it. Not bad that 'warm hutch of forgetfulness' and yet it was damned difficult to forget entirely ... must be too practical, too aware of consequences. But who the hell would be able to forget ... when even the bed one was sleeping on was paid for by *her*. Everywhere he looked she was there in some material manifestation. In a life like mine the shackles are always there. Even in my arms she is Sally White from The Fulham Bazaars and I am George and getting fat and to-morrow will be Sunday with fatter papers.

He sat down at the table in front of the lobster salad he had prepared. The single candle in the centre of the table cast sparkling reflections on the dark polished surface.

'His lordship's being very quiet this evening. Can I join in?'

'I was thinking about the warm hutch of forgetfulness ...'

'You sound just like a book ... Did you make it up?'

She was so unspoilt, so spontaneous ... George didn't feel that he could boast...

'Read it in some magazine I think.' How many men would have sacrificed the reward of merited admiration?

'Oh, the lobster is good, it really is ...' She leant across the table intimately. Her words seemed wrapped in a seductive softness. How well she had done her hair and that frilly dress ... takes one back a bit. Suddenly he had an idea, he got up and walked over to the sideboard. From the bowl of roses there he picked out a particularly dark-red bloom and breaking off the stalk near the top came up behind her.

'Shut your eyes,' he murmured; she obeyed. Deftly he slipped the rose into the soft hollow between her small breasts. She opened her eyes and looked down modestly.

'You are in a funny mood tonight.'

'Staid old George can get up to some pretty good tricks, eh? ... You wouldn't think it, but I once got a bit tight and pretended to commit suicide to scare them all.' He sat back and nodded as though with satisfaction.

'You never ... I mean, they must have gone off their heads ... Weren't they hopping mad when they discovered?'

'No, they took it pretty well. You should have seen Ruthie ... cried like a baby ... I can tell you, there's been no trouble since then.'

If only fiction could become fact. Still at least Sally would never know. There she was only a couple of feet away ... Her skin above the black dress looked brilliantly white, emphasised by the deep colour of the rose. Just like an old-fashioned Valentine with the lace and the rose. Her arms looked like the slender limbs of a young girl ... Must have had too much wine, getting maudlin ... George jerked himself back to reality with the sudden awareness of a young and naked body beneath her dress. Not even that could entirely blot out Ruth and Trelawn, but they certainly seemed further away.

In the sitting-room with Sally on his knee they had drifted still further. As his lips touched her grape-smooth cheek and the circle of her surrounding fragrance overwhelmed him, he forgot. The soft pastel shades of the room seemed infinitely restful and delicate. The warmth of the fire kissed the dove-grey carpet; the lilac curtains blotted out the street.

Ten minutes must have passed ... George heard the incongruous jangling of the door bell from another world. Would he answer it? There might have been an accident in the street ... a fire in another flat ... no alternative. Sally got up from his knee ...

'Won't be a moment.'

The Angel of Death would have been more welcome to George than the sight before him. He started back as though from the deadliest of vipers. Where was Moses now ...?

The street lamps gave off a dim light but this spectre was all too apparently human. David's breath came in small steamy clouds clearly visible in the cold night air. David smiled.

'I didn't like to telephone because ...'

In a flash of apocalyptic light George saw what had to be done ... the only thing ... his breath came more easily ... the stone in his stomach weighed less. His legs were no longer wax under a tropical sun. He was aware of the existence of his tongue again.

'You must be famished ... long journey ... nice little pub round the corner ... ham sandwiches ... back in a minute ... wait here.'

'But I've just eaten and anyway I'm under age for pubs. I can't drag you out at this hour of night having just turned up on you without a word. If I can just come in for a moment I'll explain ...'

David looked at George with alarm ... he had obviously been drinking. It really was just his luck to have come on one of his nights. He went on anxiously:

'It's all quite simple, you see ...'

'Of course it's simple ... now look, no nonsense ... I know you haven't eaten ... just being polite ... no need for that ... I'll be back ...'

George floundered back into the flat through a wall of water ... at last he saw the sitting-room door.

'Behind the sofa ... disaster ... no time ... I'll ... later . . you can come out when you hear the door,' he whispered incoherently.

He'd left open the flat door. He saw the sitting-room door was open too. She was about to speak ... how loud? ... must stop her. She was standing a good six feet away ... nothing for it. He dived towards her and caught his foot on the edge of one of the white Chippendale chairs. The thick dove-grey carpet absorbed a good deal of the noise, but not all.

She was struggling fiercely as they both hit the ground ... George got a hand over her mouth. He started to drag her behind the sofa. She was kicking out viciously with her high-heeled shoes. One of them flew off, narrowly missing his head. He pinned her down safely out of sight. Her eyes were wide with horror. He must have gone mad. Oh God ... George was hissing at her with a finger over his mouth, then he was whispering again.

'He's here ... outside ... here ... stay ... I'll explain ... later.'

Sally obeyed with the blind terror of an animal hypno-tised with fear. George emerged from behind the sofa still on his hands and knees. He felt desperately weak. Suddenly he saw the shoe in the middle of the floor. With the last supreme effort he hurled himself on top of it. He looked up just as David appeared in the doorway.

'I heard a noise so I thought you must have fallen down ... and when you didn't come back I felt I'd better ...'

David's alarm redoubled as he saw George writhing across the floor evidently trying to reach an arm-chair.

There was one thought in George's mind: he had to get rid of the shoes under a chair. With his back to David he managed to do so undiscovered.

He might be having a fit ... what did one do when people had fits? But George made a miraculous recovery. He was on his feet again. David saw a nasty-looking cut on his fore-head; he must have done it when he fell. He'd never seen him so bad before.

'Are there any bandages in the house?'

'About that little pub ... really very close ... a bit of elastoplast and I'll be fine.'

'No,' said David with authority. 'You've had a great deal too much already.'

George sank into an arm-chair and fired his last shot: 'Well, if you won't let me have a little brandy at the pub you'll have to go to the all-night chemists at Piccadilly Circus and get me a sedative. I'll never sleep otherwise.'

David was shaking his head. Quite suddenly George was crying; the effort, the shock, the pain, the indignity had all overcome him. What was there left? He felt himself the prisoner in the dock just before the black cap is put on. Nothing could save him now. If only it could all be over. The tears had stopped.

'You must understand, I can't leave you here in this state. You've already hurt yourself badly enough ... I should never forgive myself if something worse happened to you.'

'David, I beg you to leave me.'

David looked at him dubiously. These flashes of sobriety were almost more worrying than his drunken writhing.

George saw what he was thinking as clearly as if he had spoken it. In despair he said:

'Will you help me to bed?'

With luck Sally might be able to escape while they were upstairs. He would throw the bedclothes about and make as much noise as he could. It would be expected of him.

'I think you'd better stay here and rest a bit before we do anything else. I'll tidy up a little while you sober up.'

He could make a dash for the door. David saw the direction of George's gaze. He saw there was no key in the lock. Instead he moved a chair in front of the door and sat on it. He had seen what George did when his mother got drunk, so the situation, short of violence, presented few problems.

George sank back deeper into his chair, his heart-beats seemed to be coming slower. At last there really was nothing he could do. David picked up an empty glass; suddenly his eye lighted on another. Not surprising; when he was this bad he might keep glasses at opposite sides of the room to save him the effort of moving. He righted the upturned chair and straightened the rucked-up carpet. A cushion lay on the floor just in front of the sofa. He went across and replaced it. He looked round the room to see if there was anything else ... wait a second wasn't that a black cushion with lace trimmings just behind the sofa ... without bothering to move he leant forward and plucked at it ... funny ... must be caught under one of the legs. He took a couple of steps and bent down ... Sally's face was about six inches from his.

For a moment neither of them moved, but remained staring at each other crouched on their hands and knees. George buried his face in the side of his arm-chair. If only he could be struck blind and deaf. In the following seconds he would rather Sally had been struck dumb. Slowly she got up, awkwardly balancing on one high-heeled shoe. Her hair had fallen down over one eye, on her left cheek there was an ugly purple swelling, and the lace had come adrift from the bottom of her skirt where David had pulled it. George's hands were over his face now, through a gap in his fingers he could see that she was trembling. Her high-pitched laughter was far worse than the abuse that George was expecting. Her whole body was shaking as each new wave overcame her. From the floor David looked up at her flung-back shoulders and the overhang of her quaking breasts. He remained immobile as in a nightmare. The first view of those green-shaded eyes still lingered before him. The shattered silence might have been his mind. Suddenly his strength returned, his legs jerked straight under him, his back unbent. As the tears started to blind him, he leapt towards the door. He half saw George's hunched form in the arm-chair as the room raced by. In his nostrils the smell of cheap scent almost stifled him. In the corridor the laughter was fainter; in front of him was an open door, he ran through it and fell in the darkness on to a large double bed. The sheets were already pulled back.

In the sitting-room, Sally had stopped laughing. She

wiped the tears from the corners of her eyes with her sleeve. At last George spoke.

'I think you'd better go.'

'I don't think it will make much difference.'

'I'd still rather you did.'

'So you're going to try and stop him running back to Mummy, is that it?'

'I just think it's only fair on the boy for you to leave us alone tonight.'

'Anybody might think it was your son the way you're going on. If he's old enough to wear long trousers, he's old enough to know about the birds and bees. Or does he think his mother and you talk about the state of the nation when you're in bed?'

'I don't know what he thinks. I just want you to go.'

All traces of Sally's laughter had disappeared.

'I suppose you're going to tell me that it was all my fault in a minute, that I've ruined fifteen years of adulterous bliss. Did you think I was going to pretend to be your washer-woman playing a quiet game of hide-and-seek with little Georgy Porgy before beddy bies? I really think you want to go back to that old bag.'

'I don't know what I want to do, except that I want to be left alone.'

'You may not realise it, but this evening's little romp has set you free. You didn't even have to lift a finger.'

She was smiling at him now. George wondered what she was thinking. Better not disillusion her now.

'I'll have to see how things work out.'

'You astound me, you really do. Little Lord Fauntleroy has met the wicked fairy so Prince Charming misses his cue.' She moved across the room towards his chair and knelt down on the floor next to him. 'Think of what we'll be able to do now. It won't be once a month but every day. It isn't too late.' She leant over intimately and slipped a hand into his shirt. Playfully she started to stroke the hairs on his chest.

George smiled back. There was no alternative he would have to play along if he was ever to get her out.

'We'll be able to go to the Riviera and Italy. I've never been abroad.' Her eyes were shining. Streaks of eye shadow lined her cheeks where she had wiped her eyes with her sleeve.

George saw visions of a fat man in Bermuda shorts walking across crowded beaches, following his typist love. They wouldn't even be able to afford Margate. Thoughtfully Sally picked the rose out of her bosom and put it in her hair. Or was it to be sunny Spain with the gay clicking of castanets? Was she thinking of the ideal bikini or dry martinis under large multi-coloured umbrellas? There'd be snapshots to show her friends, or perhaps a ciné camera. Pictures of George swimming, lounging, drinking, driving, George draped over a crumbling pillar by the Parthenon. Of course he'd take pictures too, of her. Sally bronzed, Sally half-naked, Sally eating caviare.

'Darling, why don't you come round tomorrow and then we'll plan something definite?'

She nodded assent. George hurried into the hall to find her coat. He scrabbled under the other arm-chair for her missing shoe.

The taxi only took three minutes. She kissed him before she got in,

'George darling, I can't remember ever feeling happier.'

❧

Hastily George shut the front door and hurried back into the flat. He was relieved to see that David had shut the bedroom door. At least he would be saved convincing him that he had merely been trying to get rid of Sally.

David was sitting on the edge of the bed. He seemed to have partially recovered. But his face was tight as a skin-stretched mask. Neither of them spoke for several minutes, then like a triggered machine David stuttered:

'How could you, how could you, how could you?'

George didn't reply.

'She was so common, so awful. How could you do it when you knew that?'

How to explain to somebody barely fifteen that proletarian flesh felt the same and young proletarian flesh sometimes better. How could he ever be judged by his peers? Who but over-sexed and fattening men dependent on elder women had a right to condemn? Hadn't he paid the price with his freedom? Shouldn't there be some reward?

'Did you love her? Could you ever have loved somebody like that?'

What to say? I lusted hopelessly?

'Once.'

'But mummy, you didn't tell mummy. Then back at home she still thought that you loved her, while all the time you hated her.'

'How could I tell her?'

'I don't know, I don't know. I only wish that I'd never come, that I'd never seen this.'

Why couldn't it have been Steven? Then it would have been straightforward damnation. There would have been no attempts to understand.

'I've always loved your mother most. I've just been weak.'

'Did you ever try and stop seeing that woman?'

'Yes, but I loved her too, in a different way. When you're older perhaps you'll understand that there are different kinds of love, some more beautiful than others.'

'So you knew you were harming a more beautiful love?'

'I couldn't help it. But now I promise you it's over.'

'You'll never see her again?'

'Never.'

'But how will you ever be able to talk to Mummy without feeling guilty?'

'I have got to learn to try again. If she ever knew, it would kill her.'

'Can you do it, though, after what's happened? Don't you want to go away with that other woman?'

'I can't cut off fifteen of the most valuable years of my life because I've been stupid once.'

'So I've got to forget tonight?'

George nodded.

'How can I? How can I?' David started to cry again. 'And

you may only be saying all this for her. You want to leave us, you want to, I know you do.'

'I swear I don't.'

'I don't know what to do. I don't ...' his sobbing increased, 'I may have to tell her.'

'She'll never get over it. My suffering, if I go back, would be nothing to hers if I don't.'

George heard the telephone dimly, he walked over to answer it. Soon the sound of Mrs. Crofts' voice jarred his ear.

David half-listened; nothing mattered any more. But George made no mistakes. Snatches of broken conversation came to David.

'...well as can be expected ... time will tell ... back in a couple of days ... no trouble having him ... David's visit has meant a lot ... being a bachelor is a lonely business ... tell him you called ... phone his mother myself ... Good-bye.'

George turned back to David.

'I don't suppose it matters why you didn't tell me you were coming. I think I can guess. And Steven gave you the address, it would have to be Steven, wouldn't it?'

'I don't see how you can blame him. How could he have known about this?'

'I'm sorry David, I'm very sorry.' George paced over to a chair and sat down. No more to be said. He glanced over the carpet towards the edge of the bed and David's feet.

'You've torn your trousers.'

'In the park coming.'

'Shuts at six.'

'I climbed.'

'Ah.'

They heard the noise of some people in the street slamming car doors, and laughing. A long silence followed. Finally George got up and said quietly, as though pained at the sound of his voice.

'I'll get a bed ready for you.'

'What time is it?'

'Only eleven.'

All that in half an hour. A life ruined in half an hour.

Just thirty minutes of hysterical indignity. George got up and moved slowly towards the door. His feet felt strangely detached.

When he got back David looked embarrassed.

'You see, after what's happened, I don't feel I can stay the night here. I'd rather catch the last train for Exeter.'

The ultimate rejection ... Oh Absalom, my son, my son. George said: 'But where would you stay?'

'There's a fairly cheap hotel near the station.'

Birds have their nests ... The whole situation was getting too ridiculous to be taken seriously. With an effort George returned the answer expected by reality:

'You can't possibly do that.'

'If you won't take me I shall have to catch a taxi.'

Reality was clearly not to be taken seriously. George went to collect his overcoat.

As they drove towards Paddington a thin sleet started to fur the windscreen.

'It usually does something when I go back to school.'

'This is the first time we've ever had sleet.'

David didn't answer. George went on:

'My wiper isn't working as well as yours.'

He looked anxiously at David; he thought he saw a weak smile.

'You mustn't tell her, really she'd never get over it.'

George hoped that David's silence was consent. A slight thread of hope seemed held out before him. Perhaps if he walked carefully, very carefully, he might survive.

They arrived at the station with five minutes to go.

'Do you want anything to read?'

'No, thank you.'

'Anyway, I expect the bookstalls are shut.'

'Do you mind if I get in now?'

'Yes, but I suppose you must.'

As George watched the train spinning out its twin spidery threads of gleaming metal, he wondered whether he ought to have felt like crying. Perhaps just one tear would redeem him, blot out what had happened. 'Blood from a stone, blood from a stone,' he muttered as he walked towards the barrier. Must be shock. He felt momentarily reassured of his humanity.

'Can I see your ticket, please?'

'I've been seeing somebody off.'

'That's what they all say.'

'How much?'

'Fourpence.'

'They've gone up.'

The ticket collector nodded and once more ducked back behind the barrier of his evening paper. George wandered towards the main exit. Not even the ticket collector wanted to talk to him. No cause for anger though; only shouldn't wounds like his leave some mark, some visible proof of suffering that elicited instant sympathy? A severe shock could change the colour of a man's hair overnight. Involuntarily, he raised a hand to his head. A truck carrying heaped-up mail bags passed a few feet in front of him; he hardly noticed it. Although there was barely a handful of people left in the station, piped music still echoed spongily over the microphones across the dank emptiness. George halted for a moment. How could he go back to the flat now to see the cushions just where David had replaced them? How could he bear to inhale the still-lingering fragrance of Sally's scent? Only with company could he lighten the burden. How many hours, how many minutes till he would be able to find a temporary solution in sleep? He looked hopefully around him for a protective confessor and comforter. To his right a tramp was being turned off a near-by bench. A man with a watering-can was sprinkling the ground in front of the Ladies' Room. Nobody else was visible in that normally crowded vastness.

No good staying here. Mechanically George's feet moved under him. The pubs would be shut by now. Nothing for it but a night club. Hadn't been to one for years; Sally didn't like them ... Sally—he thought of the morning and the inevitable breaking of his promises. There really was worse to come. When he had reached the entrance and walked out into the covering night, he felt safer. Tomorrow might come, but now, now at least in the few hours of tranquillity that remained to him, couldn't he live a little still? By himself probably not, but with assistance it should be possible. He had a right didn't he, as much as any man did, to forget the inevitably sobering dawn? What's done is done, no good crying over ... crying, out of the question, too numbed, too cold for that sort of thing. But why not? Because *he* was the real victim? A wave of acute self-pity made George shiver. David would get over it; but he might very well never recover, certainly materially it would be the end of the road if the news reached home. His teeth were chattering, grimly he fixed his jaw. The snow felt cold and wet on his forehead. On the streets in weather like this without even the consolation of being able to play the violin. Visit Father Christmas in his fairy cave under the railway bridge. There wouldn't even be the money for the uniform. The cold seemed to seep with a slow and agonising numbness through his shoes. But inside in the warmth, in the dark, with a large deep glass of brandy ... while David was alone in that train ... when tomorrow Sally would come and after that when he had been rejected ... Was it the melting snow or were they, could they be tears? If so, tears of what? George didn't think, as he blundered on towards the car. Inside the club the warmth would be so warm, the darkness so protecting, the brandy so forgetful.

After almost eight years' absence, George had not forgotten the way to *The Naked Angel*. As soon as the windscreen wipers had pushed aside the snow, he let out the clutch and accelerated.

In his empty third-class compartment, David gained small consolation from the feeble reading lights muffled by their dusty faded shades. Outside the countryside fled by in its cold and dark indifference. At last he got up and pulled down the blind. Still standing, he reached into his coat pockets and produced a crumpled ten-shilling note and a few coppers. Not enough for a hotel and there was no chance of going back to the school in the middle of the night. He flopped down into his seat and tried to sleep. But closed eyes were no defence against the pictures of the mind. Sally was still with him, her eyes, her smell, but worst of all her laughter. And all the time he was returning to the unfeeling world of 'flu and football boots, half-eaten sardine tins and echoing corridors. Then there would be the unenthusiastic bickerings of Hotson and Chadwick. Whom could he tell? The morning's sunshine seemed as far away as the previous term. His walk through the park might have happened to somebody else. How could anything ever be the same again for any of them? And yet it would have to be. Perhaps George was right, to say nothing might be the only way. But was it possible not to break down and tell her everything. If only there were somebody else to ease the load, but there was nobody ... nobody ... nobody ... The rattling of the train seemed to re-echo the word over and over again.

If only she had been a little like Mummy, only a very small bit. But she had been so terrible, vulgar and common. Her voice, everything about her had been awful. He could still almost hear the harshness of her laughter. How would he be able to go on living at home seeing his mother deceived? If George couldn't see how much better she was, then he didn't deserve going on being near her. Perhaps he really didn't want to. But what would she do without him, what could she do? His thoughts turned to the night in front of him in the cold of an unknown waiting-room. What did I do so wrong to deserve all this. What did I do? His breath began to come in starts. With his head cradled in his hands he gave in to the rhythm of the train as the tears came. Bent almost double, he felt his chest swelling until the bursting pain wrung each individual sob from the centre of his body.

She hadn't been a perfect mother, but so much better than he had ever felt till now. Remembered presents, smiles and kisses broke the words from him unsummoned: 'Mummy, oh Mummy.' How would he be able to speak to her again without pain if he didn't say what he knew? The remorse less jolting and clattering of the train dulled his thoughts. There seemed no possible answer.

Some minutes later the guard saw him from the corridor, small and crumpled in his corner seat. He slid back the door.

'Nothing wrong is there, son?'

'Nothing,' said David looking away trying to hide his tears. 'I'm going back to school.'

'Somebody meeting you at this hour of the night?'

'Yes.'

'Well, we've all had to go to school, like it or not. You'll feel better when you're back with your mates. If you want to sleep I'll wake you. Where are you getting off?'

'Exeter, thank you, thank you very much.'

Gently the guard shut the door again. David's tears started once more. Why did he have to be so kind?

The train was coming into Reading, hardly a third of the way. Opposite David was a map. The track ahead of him stretched on for miles under its deepening cover of snow.

It was just after three o'clock in the morning; George was sitting in the flat opposite a ratlike-looking man. Between them on the carpet was an empty bottle: on top of the neck a pile of matches rested precariously. The rat was speaking nasally.

'Your turn, old man.'

George jerked out of his chair. He picked another match out of the open box; holding it gingerly by one end, he lowered it slowly towards the matches on top of the bottle. Just as he was about to let it go, he faltered, flicked his hand away again. Beads of perspiration stood out on his forehead. The bottle was quivering too much. He held his hand out in front of him. Funny, that seemed firm enough. He sensed his opponent's eyes on him, willing him to make a mistake. He looked beyond the bottle to where an alien pair of black shoes rested on the carpet; above them rose a pair of trousers. George looked no higher than the knees. His eyes fell back to the bottle again; taking a deep breath, he once more lowered his hand. Lower, lower, until the match was touching the pile. He dropped it and let out his breath in a long hiss of disappointment. The pile slipped slightly to one side before slowly toppling to the floor. George's hand groped blindly in his breast pocket. Another pound note was extracted and handed over.

'You don't want to stop, old man?'

Never, never. George nodded violent disagreement. Of course it was ludicrous to be gambling with a total stranger on a night like this. The man had given him a number of drinks at the club, but that hardly explained the indignity of his present position. How the hell had he been talked into it? All that brandy and now this, 'Just to see who's got the steadiest hand.' My God. Yet to stop now ...

'I'll go on,' came his proud if indistinct words.

They repeated the exercise several times more, alternately placing matches on the bottle-neck. George lost another three times.

'Just the luck of the game,' said the man complacently.

Giving money to strangers; must be out of my mind. George angrily splashed out another whisky for himself. A lot went on the table. Didn't even know the fellow's name. If he knew what that money meant, what robbery it was, it would burn a hole in his suit. Like robbing a child, no better than that.

Both men were sitting in silence now. The chair gave a warning jolt under George. Mustn't doze. At least that bloody game had made him forget how drunk he was. He fixed his eyes on one of the flower prints to steady the room. The floor steadied but the wall still pulsated intermittently like a living thing. George looked at the hairs on the backs of his hands as they rested on the arms of his chair. His feeling of nausea grew: disgust with himself, disgust with his body, disgust that he'd asked such a little worm back. And what had they done at that club? Drunk too much and talked about women like a couple of sex-starved adolescents.

Absolutely nothing in common. What did he want to know about anybody else anyway? Wasn't what he knew about himself bad enough? He took another gulp from his glass. A bit dribbled down his chin. He looked across the room: the little sod wasn't even drinking. George got up with difficulty. He forced his features into a smile. The result was diabolical.

'Have another, won't you?' he leered.

'Think I'll pass this time actually, old thing, if that's all right. Doctor's orders and that sort of thing.'

'As you like.' George gritted his teeth. Namby-pamby little swine. His own glass was empty; uncertainly he stumbled over to the drinks table. He sensed a cold pair of piggy eyes following him.

'I hope I'm not being an old busybody or anything like that, but do you think you ought to have any more?'

'Yes.'

George's head was throbbing, his eyes felt as though they were being pressed forwards from inside his skull. Wouldn't be able to hold it back much longer. What right had he got, wasn't his drink. Anyway why the blazes shouldn't he know? It'd make him feel the worm he was for taking that money. He looked at his small, dark, darting eyes, and his thin little nose. Nothing generous or big-hearted there. Even his mouth was mean. Lips like a thin pair of rubber pincers ... pretty good that. George dwelt on the neatness of his tie knot. Bet he has his nails done too. No dirt anywhere, no revelations. Just a tidy mistress somewhere and a bit of vicariously prim sex in night clubs as a change. Only silence now. Silent night, holy night, even down to the snow. What a marvellous final celebration. Tell him; that would make him sit up a bit. George's mouth opened; slowly but distinctly the words formed,

'I suppose you think I own this place?'

The man looked puzzled.

'Or rented it. Look, I'm afraid I don't quite see what ...'

'Well, I can tell you; I don't, not one thing. Everything's paid for by her. Tables, chairs, curtains, teaspoons; she doesn't know it, even the lavatory seat's hers.'

George dimly heard him cough. Must have embarrassed him. He was probably thinking gents don't say things like that. Damn fine specimen him ... having his nails done. At last the answer came.

'Terribly sorry.'

George hardly heard. Sorry for what anyway? Hadn't told him; must have guessed. What did he know about it? About the long-tolerated familiarity that didn't even breed contempt.

'It was just the money. Seduced by silks and satins. Despicable isn't it?'

The man seemed sunk in contemplation. George was beginning to feel sleepy. Everything was slowing down now. No more surprises. Anger seemed so unreasonable. He heard the man speaking.

'Looking at it realistically, what have you and I got?'

'Twenty years.'

'More, more I'm afraid. Depressing but true. Thirty years of fatty degeneration and restraining garments if you care. And have you ever thought of making it less? ... Well, exactly. When it actually comes to it the ground looks too far away, the water too cold and the sleeping-pills too cowardly.'

The sing-song sadness of his voice made George feel more sympathetic. Wasn't that how *he* felt? Even the most unlikely humans had a mystical bond. Everybody ought to try and help his neighbour.

'I suppose one must try and learn to start again.'

'Would we could. No, oh dear me no; not a chance of that. Far too late. No good running after the last bus ten years after it's gone. Just a matter of waiting. Somebody might die possibly, if you wait long enough. You could even try somebody else if you felt up to it. You've retained most of your teeth and lost little of your hair.'

'But I've lost my initiative. I've been tamed.'

'Even domestic animals have a remarkable talent for finding new homes and new feeders.'

George nodded his head sadly. How nice it would be to agree.

'But they can get up on their hind legs and beg. What can I do? I'm not black so I can't be a bus conductor.'

'How about starting a prep. school?'

'Can't even do that without capital. And when there's nothing else left I won't even be able to listen to the Daily Service on the radio.' The petals of his self-pity opened still wider. He didn't notice the growing look of disdain on the other's face. Lugubriously he went on: 'If you'd been tempted as I was, lived through what I did, you'd have done the same. A hero's reward, a place in paradise for the asking with no strings attached ... a country house, the chance of a London flat and money, money, money. No more worrying. Would you have refused in my place?'

'I'm not you and nobody offered.'

'I can't even drink without money.'

'Look, about that money; I'm quite prepared to give it back.'

George hesitated before refusing.

'Quite out of the question,' he murmured sadly. There were limits after all. Limits to what? To suffering, to indignity? He felt suddenly poetic.

'I loved and was abused,' he said loudly.

'Better than never to have loved,' came the softer answer.

'I gave, but my gift was rejected.'

'There was nobody to whom I could give.'

George heard his voice at last ringing with the wisdom of ages:

'To have something and then to see it snatched away is the worst that any man can suffer.'

'Worse than never to have and never to hope for?'

'Only words,' George muttered from his great eminence. Suffering did things to a man, it was true; ennobled him. There was no point in saying more. He hiccupped slightly.

'I think I'm going to bed now,' he said.

'Mind if I stay the night?'

'Do, please do,' George's smile was almost seraphic as he rose before leaving the room.

As soon as George had gone, the man got up and went

over to a suitcase that had been intriguing him for some minutes. The feminine name on the side could hardly be that of the occupant of the flat. Yet there was certainly nobody else around. Deftly he opened it. On the top was an envelope: 'To darling George from Sally.' He frowned. George had told him his name was Simon at the club. Next he fished out a brassière. The woman it belonged to was clearly not a fat one. A pair of frilly black pants seemed to indicate that she was not an old one either. He pursed his lips and started to whistle. Idly he flicked the brassière into his hand with his toe.

At that moment George reappeared in the doorway.

'I'd rather you put that down.'

'I don't think you've been quite fair you know, telling me that lie about your name. For all I know everything you've said may have been part of an enormous practical joke.'

'I can assure you it was not at your expense. Good night.'

George had spoken wearily, and it was with an effort that he went back to his bedroom. He felt numbed rather than drunk. He didn't want to see or hear anything else for a long time. Laughter and tears both seemed so unlikely now. He sank down on to the bed fully dressed and for that brief moment before sleep came he knew what it was to feel and understand nothing.

Sleep came in the drawing-room too. Two hours later the man woke up feeling cold and stiff. He stretched and laboriously heaved himself out of his chair. The sound of George's regular breathing was the only noise in the stillness. He crossed the room to the windows and drew the curtains. The snow had stopped, but even in the darkness he could sense that the sky was still heavy. Not a single star shone through. The snow had settled on the street lamps too, dimming their light. He shivered slightly, then turned away from the window and went out into the hall. On a chair he saw an overcoat. It was too dark to gauge its colour. He couldn't remember bringing a coat, except of course with it being so cold he would hardly not have done so. His arms slid easily into George's silk-lined sleeves. Soon he had quietly closed the flat door behind him and was walking noiselessly away down the muffled street.

Sally was wearing a blue cape with a large buckle that fastened just below the chin. Her knee-length otterskin boots effectively kept out the cold dampness of the snow underfoot. Eagerly she scuffed her way towards the tube station.

Sitting in the train she caught sight of her reflection in the window opposite. The cape and the boots were only a few days old. She looked around her at the other women in the carriage; there was no doubt about it, she was better-looking than any of them; perhaps better than any woman in the train. A man standing on the other side of the carriage was looking at her tartan-stockinged knees. Demurely she covered them with her handbag, lowering her eyes at the same time. The cape really suited her enormously.

How lucky it was that George had never been able to marry that woman, she thought with satisfaction. There would be no divorce or anything squalid like that. They would be able to go away at once for a nice long rest. Rome, Paris, New York, the names sounded so much better than they ever had before. Stewards, and pilots, take-off and touch-down, crowded streets, sunshine, parasols, piazzas. She smiled with this new delight in her situation. Nobody else in the train on a Sunday morning would be able to entertain such thoughts.

She looked up to see that they were coming into a station. She had missed the right one. But what did it matter if she missed the next?

In her otterskin boots the distance did not deter her. As she left the station, she slipped on a pair of dark-blue gloves that matched her cape.

It was almost eleven o'clock; George was bound to be up. She hurried along clean white streets, not yet dirty grey with churned-up slush. Each individual railing spike had a little cap of snow. She crossed a road; on the corner was a pillar-box; playfully she scooped some snow off the top. Her gloved hand left a neat cut of red. She threw the snow on to the ground hastily. Might mark her gloves. She could see a pale sun shining behind the trees of a garden to her right. One more street to go.

In the flat George lay on his back in bed snoring softly. His mouth was hanging open. He hadn't drawn the curtains the night before, so the wan sun softly lit the room. George's clothes were lying in an untidy heap on the floor. An open cupboard door revealed a number of suits and a cluster of ties on a rail.

His snoring was still the only noise in the flat. Church bells were ringing in St. Cuthbert's at the end of the street.

George woke up suddenly. He shook his head violently to try and get rid of the noise; but it went on. Another second and it had stopped. He pulled himself up into a sitting position. His mouth felt terribly dry. The bell was ringing again. He swung his feet on to the floor and looked around helplessly for a dressing-gown. Where the hell was it? Useless. If he could only find a coat to cover his nakedness. He had vague memories of having left one in the hall. He went out but there was no sign of it. The hall felt unbearably cold. He could go into the bedroom and cover himself with a blanket. George looked at the door of the flat. He only had to walk a few feet and open it. That was all. He stood in the middle of the hall as though turned to stone. No, he wouldn't answer it. She could ring and ring and ring, till the bell gave up or her finger froze to it. He went back into the bedroom and got into bed. The bell rang once more and then all George could hear was his breathing and the bells of St. Cuthbert's. Sleep was impossible now. He lay there warm but restless.

Sally's boots flipped through the snow as she ran on, slithering, sliding. She ran past the gardens, this time to her left, she raced past the pillar-box where the little red wound showed as clearly; the white-capped railings blurred in a continuous line of white and black.

At last she saw a taxi, she gave an address and then, throwing herself down on the seat, burst into tears.

'The bastard, the bastard.' But it wouldn't be the end of it, oh no. He couldn't go crawling out of it like that. She had trusted him and he had deceived her; deceived a simple unsophisticated girl. She beat the leather seat with her small clenched fists. Her feet drummed on the floor of the cab. She looked down at her otterskin boots, 'Horrid things, I'll never wear them again. I'll burn my cape and my gloves.'

She was nearly home when she had an idea. Once again she was smiling and this time it was not with innocent joy and anticipation.

EIGHT

F R A N T I C exertions with brushes and spades had ensured that the Finals of the House Rugby Competition would take place.

Crofts was standing on the touchline in front of a dirty bank of slush and snow. His overcoat was pulled up well round his neck. He opened his mouth as wide as he could.

'Co——me on, Greville,' he roared hoarsely. It had been seven years since the house had got to the finals and even then they had been beaten. Winning the competition would be extremely good for house morale and might well be the beginning of better things. Crofts's mouth opened again.

'Let's have another try, Greville.'

He looked around him with disapproval at the ranks of junior boys in his house. Perhaps it had not been a good idea to make it compulsory to watch the match. So far he had been the only person to cheer.

Cold hands had meant fumbled passes and to date David had not touched the ball. He was wishing that he had put on two vests. Patiently he waited for another scrum to form. Almost all sensation seemed to have left his fingers. Suddenly the scrum-half had the ball away. David saw it coming down the line towards him. He took it well on the run. Three of the opposing forwards were running round to cut him off. He swerved and went on running. His breath was coming in rushes. One of them got a hand to his vest but he wrenched himself free. He handed off another in the face with all his strength.

Ahead of him he could see the posts and the solitary figure of the full back (full back for the school). David ran straight at him. Not much further if only he could get past. He glanced behind. Nobody there. Have to go on. At the last moment he pretended to slip, swerved and he was through.

'Played Lifton, played,' yelled a distant Crofts. A thin cheer rose from the chilled spectators. David got up slowly, mud all over the front of his body; he walked back with the ball for a few yards before tossing it to Hotson, who was going to try and convert.

David trotted down the field again and turned in time to see Hotson's massive kick rise high between the posts. There was another slightly weaker round of applause.

Over on the far touchline, David caught sight of Andrew Matthews wearing a dark overcoat and a silk scarf round his neck. Even at that distance he could tell that he was smiling. David felt enormously proud—of course it couldn't really make any difference, only somehow it undeniably did.

The game ended without further scoring. Greville had won.

Several days after, lunch was drawing to an end in Greville.

'Any more for you, Lifton?'

Crofts invitingly held out a spoonful of trifle.

'No, thank you, sir.'

'Well, you'll have some anyway, won't you, Chadwick?'

Crofts was smiling.

'I think I'm fairly full actually, sir.'

'No offers?' Spoon still poised, Crofts glanced round the table, 'I'll have a bit myself anyway.'

Every week two boys from the middle of the house enjoyed the privilege of sitting on the housemaster's table: the idea being to give the house a sense of unity. So far neither David nor Chadwick had opened their mouths. Crofts made several hopeless efforts to save the flagging conversation before finally admitting defeat. Sometimes he began to doubt his abilities as a schoolmaster. It was a rare day indeed when the conversation rose above the standard of Intermediate English for Beginners. Slowly he rose to his feet amidst the usual scraping of chairs.

'For what we have received, may the Lord make us truly thankful.'

Crofts paused respectfully before going on to other matters.

'Father Peter will be taking House Prayers this evening and will be having coffee with me afterwards. Anybody who would like to meet him would be most welcome ... confirmation candidates especially. Last time very few people came, so I hope that there will not be a similar occurrence tonight.' He paused again, then, taking a deep breath, went on: 'I'm afraid it has once more come to my notice that the lavatories are being improperly used.' The inevitable titters died away. David caught Andrew Matthews's eye momentarily. Had he winked? David looked down at the table. 'Orange peel and waste paper should be put in the receptacles provided and not down the lavatories. It only causes extra work for the cleaners. I think that's all.'

As they walked out of the room together, Chadwick turned to David, 'I do wish Crofts wouldn't clean his teeth with his tongue while he's speaking.'

Half an hour later David was sitting in the Biology laboratory writing down Mr. Fisher's words.

'Then I took a length of glass piping and covered one end with a semi-permeable membrane. I then ...'

'How do you spell that, sir?'

David relaxed gratefully and looked around him. All along one side of the room were specimens in glass jars, floating in transparent preserving fluid. Sad and isolated ... brains, eyes, intestines; rows and rows of them stared at him. In some other glass cases rested bone after bone, all of them neatly labelled, ulnas, tibias, clavicles. David didn't like biology. Worst of all was a single frog in a tank. The creature was breathing heavily as it sat in a corner, waiting to be dissected by the sixth form after a speedy execution.

Fisher droned on,

'After one week the water had risen six inches up the piping, after two, nine inches. The water to equalise the sugar content ...'

David stopped listening. Since he had returned to Edge-combe he had still been unable to come to any decision about George. School routine had not, as he had feared, made the burden more difficult to bear. It was only when left by himself that he had time to think about it. Night was the worst time, although half-days in the study with Hotson and Chadwick were none too easy. Looking out of the window he could see the main drive twisting down towards the village. He thought of the following day when Matthews was to take him out to tea. He had said nothing about it to anybody else as yet. Boys were not often taken out by masters. There was no doubt about it, it was a considerable privilege. David smiled. He looked at the frog and no longer felt sorry for it. Come to think of it, the thing looked rather like Mr. Fisher: all wrinkles and pouches.

At last the talking stopped. Everyone sat back and waited.

'For the rest of the lesson we'll do some diagrams of corms and bulbs.'

David looked at his watch; at least twenty-five minutes till he was free.

When he got back to the study Hotson and Chadwick were in the middle of an argument. David had a fair idea of what it would be about. The previous day Hotson's mother had come down to the school for the afternoon and had sat in the study long enough to force David and Chadwick into the library; a room that was as cold as it was uncomfortable.

'She could have taken you out to tea or to the cinema. But did she? She has to sit in here all afternoon.'

'Maybe she liked it,' said Hotson phlegmatically.

'Here of all places. You might have told her it was a half-day.'

David stood listening in the doorway.

'Shut up, can't you,' snapped Chadwick. 'It isn't exactly summer, in case you haven't noticed.'

Obediently David complied and went over to the table to

put his books down. He dropped them on top of a piece of butter, which he noticed just too late.

'I wish you didn't have to leave your bits of food all over the table,' he retaliated.

'Who had toast this morning?' Hotson said.

'Exactly,' Chadwick backed him up.

'All right, start on me,' said David wearily. Why did they always have to bicker? The real trouble was that they seemed to enjoy it.

While wiping the table, David was unlucky enough to knock over a bottle of orange juice. Hotson's mother was forgotten in the general reprimand that followed.

'Thank God, I shan't be here tomorrow,' said David defiantly.

'I'm almost in tears, tell me all. Is it to be the races or the Cup Final?' sneered Chadwick. 'Or perhaps another afternoon in the library?'

'Actually I'm going out to tea with Mr. Matthews.'

'Going up in the world I see,' Chadwick paused, then said more thoughtfully, 'Really, come to think of it that's quite smart.'

'No more work,' Hotson added sourly. 'I went out with a master once. Some time ago of course.'

'Of course. I'll say; when you were young and pretty I suppose. Tell us another.'

'With the art master actually,' said Hotson with dignity.

'And you weren't asked again?' said Chadwick sweetly.

Hotson grimaced.

'I ate six out of eight sandwiches.'

'A lesson for all,' said Chadwick to David.

'Has anybody ever told you, you've got real charm,' said Hotson, smiling he hoped ironically.

'Frequently.'

'You know, I don't think I can stand either of you any longer,' Hotson announced as he got up from his chair.

'You mean you've got to go for extra French,' returned Chadwick.

'I damn well don't.'

'You've changed the day?'

'Yes, if you must know.'

'Aren't you going then?'

'I've changed my mind, since you *want* me to go.'

David watched them both from over by the window. On and on and on, day after day; biology, even with frogs, was immeasurably preferable. A few minutes and they would be on about Hotson's mother again. He walked quietly towards the door.

'I think I'll go for a walk.'

'Lovely day for one,' said Hotson, glancing at the darkening window. 'And for Christ's sake shut the door,' added Chadwick.

Andrew Matthews drove a small green Morgan; old but fast. He stole a sideways glance at David sitting in the seat next to him. He liked to drive out of the school grounds at speed in second. The noise was enormous.

They were approaching the lodge gates already. Ahead of them the road curved down into the valley. The village was hidden by mist streamers which glowed golden in the afternoon sunlight. Patches of snow still shone white in the fields. David rested his hands on the dashboard to stop himself sliding sideways as they cornered into the village street. Andrew turned to him and smiled:

'Thank God for being out of the place.'

David laughed.

'I'm glad, too. Where are we going?' he added.

'A few miles yet, wait and see.'

Andrew was casually dressed in a pair of old flannel trousers and a heavy brown sweater. Just the right off-duty touch, he thought with satisfaction. He had felt a little apprehensive about what to say to David, but now after several pints with lunch it all seemed so easy. They'd talk about school of course and that ass Crofts. 'Thank God for being out of the place,' how right it had sounded and how successfully it had put him at his ease. Andrew glanced upwards momentarily at the clear blueness of the sky. The sheep on a hill to their left looked as clean and well-defined as plastic toys.

'Does it seem long since you came to Edgecombe?' asked Andrew. 'Ages and ages, I expect, even my month seems like a lifetime.'

'Years, and years, sometimes I can hardly remember having been anywhere else.'

'I hated school myself,' Andrew eagerly confided. 'I had the most awful housemaster.'

David grinned. Did he dare ask? He paused a moment before doing so.

'Worse than Crofts?'

'I don't know that I ought to be discussing my colleagues with a pupil,' Andrew said with mock pomposity.

David was not sure whether he was being serious. Better to play safe.

'I suppose not,' he said betraying his disappointment.

'Come on, I wasn't being serious. No, he was far worse than Crofts.' Andrew wondered how far he dared go. Stories did tend to get back. But David seemed upset. Anyway he'd started so had better go on. 'Crofts isn't that bad is he? Just a bit of an old fool with no sense of humour.'

'"The lavatories are being improperly used,"' David mimicked laughing.

'"The proper receptacles should be used,"' went on Andrew.

'Have you noticed that he cleans his teeth with his tongue after lunch?'

This time Andrew laughed out loud.

'Perhaps his wife doesn't give him enough to eat in the evening.'

'Chadwick says that he hasn't bought a suit for the last five years. But I suppose one oughtn't to make fun of him.'

'Quite right. I'm a schoolmaster too.'

'But not like him,' David added hastily.

'Thank you,' said Andrew smiling. Ahead of him he saw a sign 'Double Bend', he accelerated as they got nearer. David gripped the dashboard as he was thrown first across the gearlever and then against the door. In spite of himself he let out a little gasp of fear.

'Makes one grateful to be alive, doesn't it?' said Andrew calmly.

'But somebody might have been coming the other way,' said David, trying to get his own back for having so unmanfully squawked.

'I'm sorry, sir.'

David tried not to laugh at Andrew's show of sadness and contrition, but failed.

'Anyway you won't do it again.'

'Scout's honour,' chirped Andrew in his most unbroken voice.

'Good,' David returned sternly.

'How do you get on with your room-mates then? Do you put them in their place too?'

David frowned.

'I don't often get the chance, they just go on bickering the whole time.'

'Can't you change your room?' said Andrew sympathetically, responding to the more serious mood.

'No, they'd say that Mummy pulled strings or something. Last term Prindle's mother asked if he could have a bigger bed and he never heard the end of it when the thing arrived.'

'I had hell like that too,' said Andrew, making up the story as he went along, 'I lived in a study with three other people. One had a tape-recorder, one a wireless, the other a cello and I had a gramophone. It was absolute murder.'

'The worst thing of all is the food that gets left around. I can't put anything down in the place without getting grease or jam all over it.'

'I always found the smell terrible too,' said Andrew embroidering again. He had always been a day-boy and a very-well-looked-after one at that.

'Yes, the smell gets me down too; Hotson always comes in after rugger and sits round before having a shower.'

Andrew remembered David's performance of a week ago with pleasure. He had never been good at games himself.

Rather a 'swot' really; but David was the complete man, sensitive with it. Anxiously he looked at him. He should never have brought up his room-mates. It was going to be hard to get the conversation back on to a more frivolous level again. Fortunately they were coming to Coombe Bassett and the tea-rooms would provide other topics of conversation. They could talk about the other people and try and guess what they did from their clothes.

'What's this village called?' said David, breaking a few moments of silence.

'Coombe Bassett; worthy of a "Beautiful Britain" calendar photograph. Note the Gothic church and fourteenth-century cottages and over there, lichened with age, is an inhabitant...'

David tried to smile as he fought with his memory. It had been here hadn't it, about two years ago, that he, George and Mummy had come? And it had been for tea then, too.

'Is the name of the tea-rooms The Green Woodpecker?' he asked suddenly.

'Yes. Why, have you been here before? I hope the place is all right. I've only driven past myself.'

Andrew looked at him apprehensively. Perhaps the 'White Hart' at Stockhampton would have been better.

'I came here with my mother once. I can't remember what the tea was like.'

But the tablecloths had been blue-and-white check and the waitress had had a limp. George had said, 'why can't the damn woman hurry' and then he'd noticed her limp. His mother had wondered why there should be a cuckoo clock in a tea-rooms called The Green Woodpecker. 'There ought to be a woodpecker clock, oughtn't there dear.' David winced at the memory of it. She could be so stupid.

Andrew held the door open for David. A couple of steps led down into a large room filled with a number of tables. David had been right about the blue-and-white tablecloths. The cuckoo clock was still there also.

Andrew saw that he would have to give up his idea of talking about the other customers. The place was empty.

'How about the one in the corner,' he said cheerfully,

indicating a table on the other side of the room. Their feet sounded noisily on the uneven oak floorboards. The room was dark and badly lit. They sat down and Andrew leant out to draw the curtains of the window next to them.

'I could have done that,' came an irritated voice from a hatch in the middle of the opposite wall.

'Very friendly, I must say,' said Andrew. 'Anybody might think I'd spat on the table.'

He said this loudly enough to be heard. David looked over anxiously at the hatch. In his embarrassment he started fiddling with the cutlery in front of him. They waited for several minutes in silence.

'Pretty quick service,' Andrew said as loudly as before.

'I think she's a cripple,' David replied softly, hoping that this would make him lower his voice. It had the reverse effect.

'I bet the floor plays hell with her joints.'

David went on fiddling with a knife. Andrew looked at him despairingly. Crofts wasn't the only one without a sense of humour. He ought to have looked inside the place before bringing David. Enough to depress anybody he thought sourly.

At last the waitress was limping towards them. She slammed the tray down in front of them. A few biscuits and a couple of meanly buttered bits of toast was the feast that Andrew saw before him. He controlled his anger and asked whether it was possible to have a cream tea. He was told that he was lucky to get toast out of season. David seemed thoroughly indifferent. Andrew decided not to swear at her as she retreated. Instead he said to David:

'I expect I'd be bad-tempered if I had to carry trays with a limp like that.'

'Me too,' said David, less distantly. Why, why, he was asking, did he have to have been there before? Just George, Mummy and himself only two tables away. It had been summer and *they* had had cream tea. George had looked out of the same window and said, pointing at the cottages opposite, 'All very pretty but just one hydrogen bomb...' Mummy had told him not to be so silly on such a lovely day and had given him another cream-covered scone. In spite of hydrogen bombs he remembered being happy, but now everything had changed. School made one forget, but the problem was still there, just as it had been there in the train. He took a large bite out of his piece of toast. He looked up to see Andrew staring at him.

'Aren't you feeling well?' he asked softly.

'No, no, I'm all right, really. I'm an awful day-dreamer that's all.'

Then after tea they'd gone to see the house where that famous writer used to live and George had managed to knock over an ink-well that hadn't been moved since the great man died. But Mummy had been terribly apologetic to the guide, who'd said that it didn't matter. She was so good like that. David felt suddenly like crying. He pressed his nails into the palms of his hands to try and stop himself, but it was no good. He looked down at the floor as though searching for his napkin.

'It's here,' said Andrew pointing at the still unfolded triangle of white paper on the table by David's plate. As David looked up to take it his eyes caught Andrew's.

'What is it?' said Andrew gently. 'You'll probably feel better if you tell somebody.

David shook his head.

'I can't, really I can't.'

But five minutes later he did. He forgot the waitress and the hatch in the wall, he forgot to try and stop his tears. He told him about the rabbits, about last Christmas, about his mother's drinking, about Dr. Everett, about Sally.

Three-quarters of an hour later the waitress came in again.

'I'm shutting up now, so if you don't mind . . .' she nodded in the direction of the door.

Andrew desperately wanted to put his arm round him as they walked towards the door. As David stepped out into the empty street he heard the cuckoo clock mocking him,

'Cuckoo ... cuckoo ... cuckoo ...' Six times, Andrew looked at his watch. Had they really been there for two hours.

As they walked towards the car, David didn't dare look at Andrew, he didn't know whether to feel relieved or ashamed. He had been so understanding and sympathetic and yet hadn't burdened him with easy consolation or cheap words of comfort.

If only I could have said something, Andrew was thinking, as he opened the driving-seat door. But there was nothing he could say. He felt helpless, if only he had suffered as a child. The only way he could hope to show his sympathy was through physical contact and that was out of the question ... out of the question, out of the question.

It was now completely dark. After a few miles Andrew realised that he had taken a wrong turning. They would have to stop and look at a map. In the darkness Andrew groped along the shelf under the dashboard. As he leant over to David's side of the car he slipped and felt his hand fall on David's knee. He started to withdraw it but suddenly felt it clasped.

What happened next Andrew found it hard to reconstruct a couple of seconds afterwards. He had been supporting his weight with his left arm resting on the back of David's seat when he leant over. Had he meant that arm to slip? Or had he really lost his balance? As his arm had left the back of the seat and lighted on David's shoulder, Andrew's cheek touched his. David instantly snatched away his hand and recoiled against the door.

'Oh my God, my God,' moaned Andrew.

The motor was still throbbing, otherwise there was no sound. Andrew could sense David's tenseness almost physically. What could he do, pretend it hadn't happened? After all, couldn't a momentary mistake be wiped out by refusing to acknowledge it?

'Funny, I could have sworn there was a map in here. But I suppose we can ask the way at the next house.' There was no reply. Andrew went on, 'anyway, we'd better be pressing on or we'll be late for supper.'

The engine sounded louder to Andrew than it had ever done, as he let out the clutch. Ten minutes later they came to a signpost which showed them the right road. David had still not spoken. Andrew was beginning to panic. Suppose he went straight up to Crofts and said that he had been assaulted. In his present state of mind he might do anything. Andrew tried again.

'Stupid that these cars don't have interior lighting. If they did, there'd be no need for groping about in the dark looking for things.'

'I'd rather you drove a bit slower,' was the only reply he got. Andrew bit his lip. Of course he'd deny it if any allegations were made. The whole thing had been a misunderstanding, anybody presented with the facts would see that. Or would they? If there was any chance of Crofts getting to know about it, oughtn't he to get there before David? Or would that look like self-confessed guilt?

When David finally spoke he was no longer angry.

'I trusted you. After all I told you, then you go and do ... that,' he brought out after a pause. 'I feel such a fool. I really thought that I'd found somebody, but I ought to have known better. I can't touch anything without making it go wrong.'

Andrew was afraid that he was going to cry again, but he need not have worried. After another lengthy silence they were nearly at the school gates. Andrew was now in no doubt as to how David had interpreted what had happened. If he was to get any promises of silence out of him, he would have to admit that something had really taken place.

They were getting out of the car. David turned to Andrew,

'I won't tell anybody.'

Andrew fought for words to defend himself with but none came. In the end he merely nodded his head and walked away in the direction of the Common Room. How the hell would he be able to go on teaching him after this? Even if he didn't go to Crofts, mightn't it get to him through rumours?

Perhaps he would have to forestall any chances of this. Stupid boy, he was leaving him little choice.

David decided to miss supper, instead he went up to his study, where he was certain of being alone for the next half-hour. He slumped down into the best arm-chair and put his head in his hands. Strangely enough he did not feel too downcast. If this business had been humiliating and disgusting, it had shown him the way to deal with his other problem: the same way, by saying nothing. Both George and Andrew were to be spared.

Nevertheless at that moment Matthews was making his way towards the housemaster's study.

NINE

STEVEN hurried on through the fog. What had the man said? Was it second on the right or third? Must be clean out of my mind going to a party on a night like this. It could wait till tomorrow, but Christ it was three weeks since he'd gone to London and still no word. How could it have failed? And yet there had been no word from home either. Steven felt the most terrible need to speak to Robert and speak to him as soon as possible.

He stopped for a moment, swore, and then started to re-trace his steps. This must be the one. He turned and began looking at the numbers. Why did street-numbering always have to be done by lunatics? After a few more yards he noticed a number of parked cars and heard the mushy sound of dance music rising weakly from a basement.

He reached the gate and looked at a group of people in front of the door. Badly dressed men clutching badly dressed girls, moths flocking to the nearest evening candle. Turn on a gramophone and see them come slavering for bad drink and bad music. Steven arrogantly pushed his way to the front of the group to find his way barred by the man giving the party. A couple of bottle-bearing thugs were being turned away. Steven watched them shambling off.

'I don't care if you've got bishop's urine in those bottles,' the host said magnanimously to another uninvited guest. Then turning to Steven:

'I don't believe I've had the pleasure ...'

'Nor do I. Robert told me you wouldn't mind my coming.'

'Well, if Robert told you perhaps ...'

But Steven had already pushed inside. Most of the party seemed to be sitting on the stairs. He could see no sign of

Robert there, so started to pick his way down the stairs. Leaving a rustle of resentful murmuring in his wake, he finally emerged in the basement. Just one room and packed with sweating heaving bodies, Steven groaned, as he leant against the door-frame. Why couldn't Robert go to slightly more civilised parties? The drinks table was fortunately just to the left. One of the dancing masses had been good enough to leave a bottle of whisky there until he returned. A half-bottle: it fitted into Steven's pocket tidily. Steven felt better tempered as he fought his way across the room towards a sofa in front of the window. Short of hanging from the ceiling, staying in one place seemed the best and least energetic way of finding Robert. When he arrived at the sofa he was amazed to find it untenanted. He found a glass on the floor and poured himself a large one. After several more drinks a red-faced young man and his girl plumped down next to him. The girl had somehow forced her arms into a tight pair of elbow-length gloves. Steven noticed the pallid roll of flesh at the top of each glove. Still, not a bad face. He looked at her more closely as he refilled his glass: china-blue eyes and long fair hair.

'Hello, Mr. Lonely,' she slurred, looking at Steven. Then added sympathetically, 'Don't you like dancing?'

'I'm a homosexual actually,' Steven smiled charmingly.

The red-faced man cut in. 'I can't place your face.'

'Can't face yours,' said Steven, still smiling.

'I hope you're not trying to take the piss.'

'Do have some of mine,' Steven held out the whisky bottle in red-face's direction.

'Where did you get that bottle?'

'You don't have to shout. I bought it in a wine merchants.'

'I don't believe you.'

Red-face was on his feet. Steven wondered whether he was going to hit him. Probably not; didn't look the sort.

'If you think I got hold of it here, I suggest that nobody would be stupid enough to leave such precious . . .'

'Who invited you?'

But the girl with the china-blue eyes lost patience before Steven did.

'Charles, go and get me a drink, please. Be a dear.'

Steven watched him unwillingly pushing through the dancers. Then he turned to his next-door neighbour.

'Thank you, deliverer mine,' he said.

'Not at all. Anything for peace and quiet.'

'So you come to parties for it?'

'You're here too.'

Steven looked at her more appreciatively. Absently he reached for his bottle and this time didn't bother with the glass. Robert seemed infinitely remote. Probably hadn't come anyway. What the hell. Now that he was here might as well try and enjoy himself. None of Sarah's friends were likely to be there. Red-face would be back soon. Better do something.

'How about a dance before your friend comes back?'

'He bought me dinner.'

'A unique achievement. I expect I could do the same when you feel a few empty spaces.' Steven held out his hand. 'What's your name?'

'Mary.'

'Come on then, Mary.'

Feebly resisting, she allowed him to pull her up from the sofa. Over his shoulder he could see red-face, drink in hand. None too soon. Deftly he steered her towards the middle of the room. The music seemed unaccountably louder there. Just as well really, no need to talk now. Lazily Steven rested his cheek against hers. She rubbed her face against his. Slowly their mouths moved towards each other. A big gooey sweet for a good boy, thought Steven contentedly. Just at that moment through several strands of flaxen hair he caught sight of Robert. He groaned inwardly. There would almost certainly be a moral lecture tomorrow.

'Friends make me sick,' said Steven confidentially.

'Me too,' replied Mary and then, 'Give us another kiss.'

At two o'clock, Steven and Mary were walking arm in arm towards the centre of town.

'Aren't you a friend of Sarah Twiss?' Mary said unexpectedly.

Steven had been watching the uncertain homeward ditherings of a drunk on the other side of the street.

'Yes,' he said absently. 'Actually I'm her fiancé. Didn't you notice the little flap on my lapel. Written with my own hands: "ENGAGED", reserved for betrothed couples and public lavatories.'

'If I wasn't drunk I'd call you a bastard.'

'A privilege I'm not likely to enjoy,' said Steven, abruptly turning left in the direction of his college.

'Yes, I know I behaved disgustingly,' said Steven shutting the door of Robert's room behind him.

Robert returned no answer from the window-seat.

'Got any cornflakes?' went on Steven, walking over to the cupboard.

'The milk's off.'

'No bread either, I suppose, and only revolting instant coffee.'

'How did you guess?'

Steven fastened his dressing-gown girdle more securely round him. Then sitting on the arm of a chair:

'Come on then, let's be having you.'

'One day they'll take you away for crimes committed against yourself,' said Robert thoughtfully.

'I'll plead diminished responsibility and force of circumstances. You didn't honestly expect me to just sit there and get drunk all on my sweet little own? Solitary drinkers are pathetic you know.'

'And if Sarah hears about it?'

'Stop being so bloody naïve. Anyway she won't. I *had* come to ask your advice but I don't think I'll be needing it after all.'

'Give me a handkerchief. I think I'm going to wet myself with grief.'

'Who's been giving you lessons in repartee?'

'I have talked to you in the past.'

Steven got up and walked over to the fire. Flicking through Robert's invitations on the mantelpiece he said:

'I've decided to go home next Saturday and I think I'll take Sarah too.'

'Think the change of air will do her good?'

'No, just a bit of elementary blackmail. "Stand and deliver, here's my fiancée, we're very much in love." Also little brother is home for his half-term, so I feel that a word in his ear would not come amiss.'

'It'll be rather unfortunate if you can't get him to spill the beans.'

'That's a risk I'm afraid I shall have to take.'

'You might find yourself marrying her out of pique if you can't get what you want.'

Steven frowned.

'Well, there'll be a certain self-righteous pleasure in that.'

'One that might diminish with the years.'

'Haven't I told you I'm fond of her? I've been going out with her for the last four months. She doesn't annoy me. She doesn't moralise and what's more she's good in bed.'

Robert had turned his back and was looking out of the window. After a pause he said softly:

'The only thing is that you don't love her.'

'You've been seeing too many films recently. Talk to an Arab about love. If they hadn't had so much free time on their hands in medieval France...'

'Nevertheless, scientists have decided that we are what we are because of our conditioning.'

'Two undergraduates talk about the important problems in life. He felt the warm blood flowing from the wound and knew that this was life, that the throbbing pulsing reality...'

'Do shut up. Now that I've restored your self-confidence I'll be going to a lecture. That is if you don't mind. If you like I'll sport the oak so that nobody disturbs your conversation.'

'Thanks.'

When Robert had left the room, Steven went over to the

bookcase and picked out a small book: *The Collins English Gem Dictionary.* Slowly he read out loud:

' "love, (*noun*) warm affection; sexual passion; sweetheart; score of nothing; (*verb transitive*) delight in." ' His eye passed further down the definition, ' "love-bird ... loving-cup ... love-in-a-mist ..." '

He was not laughing though when he sat down on the window-seat and looked out across the quad.

'Oxford 1960, Oxford 1960,' he muttered to himself.

TEN

THE tic under his right eye seemed worse this evening. Mary Crofts looked at her husband anxiously. It really was too bad that this new man should have got into trouble so soon. Lifting the coffee-pot off the table by her chair she poured herself a cup. Crofts looked up from the essay he was reading.

'Can I have a cup?'

'You told me you couldn't sleep yesterday, so I don't know whether you oughtn't to have some hot chocolate.'

'I hate the stuff. You know quite well why I didn't sleep.'

'Well, what are you going to do about it?'

'There are various alternatives. I could just leave well alone. After all the boy hasn't said anything about it yet.'

His wife shook her head violently. Her small eyes looked more piercing than usual behind her pink-rimmed spectacles.

'And what happens if it comes to light? If the man tries it on somebody else?' she said scornfully.

'I'll just look rather stupid for believing his story.'

Mary looked at him sadly.

'It won't be the first time. You weren't exactly Edgecombe's blue-eyed boy when Bagshaw collapsed in prayers.' She stirred her coffee angrily at the memory of it. Part of it had been bad luck, but Alfred just could not judge when it came to choosing a house tutor. 'To stray neither to the right hand nor the left,' then he'd just fallen down, drunk as a newt. 'We don't want a repetition of that fiasco,' she added.

'We could ask Matthews to leave.'

'Don't be a fool, Alfred. What would that look like in the middle of term?'

'I could announce that he'd had to go home to look after his mother.'

'I suppose none of the boys would put two and two together? Besides, he might well appeal to the Head and then it would only be the boy's word against his. You'll have to get more on him than that. Anyway, Lifton hasn't said anything yet and the man is, as you never stopped telling me, a well-qualified master.'

'I could talk to Lifton and ask him why he accused the man.'

'That seems a better idea. Then you'd at least have the allegation. Why that young fool Matthews had to come to you in the first place, I can't imagine.'

Crofts got up and went over to the table in the window alcove. Picking up a packet of cigarettes he said:

'Inexperience I suppose. Didn't know that boys never let out that sort of thing. Went to a day-school himself.'

'What exactly did he think you were going to do about what he told you?'

'He just said that he thought I ought to know the real story before anybody else tried to tell me otherwise. What could I say when he said that I would know what should be done?'

'Asked him what he would do in your place. Still it's a bit late for that now. And once you've got that allegation, what then?'

Crofts lit his cigarette and rolled it back and forth nervously between finger and thumb.

'Tell him that Mr. Matthews had warned me against this malice and say that I didn't believe him. I should also say that if false accusations of this sort were made in the future I should know their source. And would act with suitable severity.'

'You think this would keep him quiet?'

'I hope so.'

Mrs. Crofts poured herself another cup and said meditatively:

'That still isn't water-tight.'

'Nothing short of getting rid of both of them is, and that, as we must already be aware, is impossible.'

'There is another way,' said Mary slowly. 'How about phoning Lifton's mother and telling her that her son has been spreading scandal. Say that you believe Matthews. Tell her the grave consequences rumours of this sort have in a house...'

'And with luck she would be so offended that she would take him away at the end of term.'

'That's the general idea. She's a temperamental woman, always complaining because her son isn't given enough personal care. His illness is an added blessing. You can say that a tough school is perhaps not best suited to such a sensitive boy. Lay the failure at the gates of the school. Sugar the pill as much as possible. "David is a highly unusual young man, whom we would hate to think of being blighted in these vital formative years", that sort of thing. Tell her that he seems unhappy too. She once told me that he used to be less withdrawn before he came to Edgecombe.'

'What if the boy said he was perfectly happy?'

'She wouldn't believe him. She's just the sort to take any excuse to keep her children at home. Don't you remember that awful fuss we had over whether his elder brother could have an umbrella at school before he got into the sixth, and how she went on about him having one at home?'

Crofts did remember it. How he'd wanted to tell her that this wasn't a nursery school but hadn't dared. She'd tried to make him admit that distinctions of this sort were childish.

'I don't like it, Mary. It's all rather underhand, and the boy's one of the best classicists we've had for years.'

'What else can you think of?'

Why the hell did he feel so fuddled these days? Crofts tried to think of another way but his mind remained empty. Eventually he nodded consent.

'I'll do it after prayers.'

ELEVEN

STEVEN saw the child coming across the compartment towards him, a large piece of orange in his hand. Steven had always been puzzled why children liked him.

'No, thank you,' he said, doing his best to smile as the infant offered him a bit.

'Come here this instant, Bobby, and leave the gentleman alone.' The mother held out a paper napkin into which her son reluctantly dropped his offering.

Steven looked at Sarah in the seat next to him. She was smiling knowingly at him. Softly she said:

'Don't you like train journeys?'

'Adore them. I just love other people's children too.'

'Sh—sh,' she reproved him gently. 'Did I tell you, darling, that I was once a waitress? I mean for a short time last vac?'

'I think you mentioned it.'

'I was always having to tell little boys not to touch the tea urns.'

Steven looked at her patiently. She always got so excited telling stories. Robert said that it was part of the freshness of her charm.

'No sir, no meringues today, I'm awfully sorry ... small boy, that tea urn's hot ... no madam, no meringues, I've just told the gentleman ... small boy I've told you already ... yeo—w ... small boy, I warned you.'

'Sh—sh,' Steven mimicked.

'You ought to have a notice on you like the tea urns,' she laughed.

Steven looked out of the window at the telegraph wires. He hadn't told Sarah about the real purpose of their visit. 'Thought you ought to meet them in case you get second thoughts.' 'But I'm not going to marry *them*.' If one knew the distance between the telegraph wires one would be able to calculate the speed of the train. His letter warning them would only have arrived this morning. George would hardly have had time to think. It would also leave him little time to brief David. Must get the truth out of the boy whatever happened. Steven set his jaw.

'What are you thinking about, Steven? You look awfully serious.'

'My chances as a maths examiner. If I knew the speed of the train I'd be able...'

'Don't tell me if you don't want to.'

'All right then. I was wondering how you're going to get on with my mother and good old uncle George.'

He'd explained away George as a virtuous gentleman companion but she was going to have to see the light soon enough. The more impartial she was to start with, the better the impression she was likely to make on his mother.

'We now accept George as one of the family,' he said ingenuously. 'He was almost a father to both of us.'

There would of course be a good deal of explaining afterwards, but Sarah's neutrality was necessary now. He might be able to get rid of her when it came to the real showdown. Tell her he had various boring things to clear up, so wouldn't she like to borrow the car for the morning and look at the countryside?

'I do hope your mother likes me,' she said earnestly. 'I'll make a great effort. I know how much it matters to you.'

If she did, if she did, thought Steven.

'They're rather unconventional, so you won't be shocked at all? It can be very boring tucked away in the country, so they do drink a bit from time to time.'

He thought of the previous Christmas and smiled. There might well be a bottle or two consumed after he left this time.

Bobby's little head was lolling across his mother's breast. Steven noticed a dribble of chocolate creeping down his little chin. He looked away but as he did so caught the mother's eye and smiled. Why did one always smile at mothers with children? A mute and patronising tribute to one's lost innocence created anew?

The train was steaming past the winter desolation of the beaches of south Devonshire. Sarah was also looking out across the empty sands.

'We always used to come to Newton Abbot for our summer holidays when Daddy was alive,' she confided. 'I met my first boy-friend there. He had a bucket with a starfish on it and used to carry around a blue telescope everywhere.'

'Most touching,' said Steven, laughing.

'It was actually,' she said primly. 'We were going to get married, only the holidays were too short to fix a date.'

'So I'm doubly lucky. I was going to marry our prep. school matron, who was fat and fifty.'

'How romantic.'

'Yes, it was actually.'

Sarah pulled the fur-trimmed collar of her overcoat up round her head, hiding her face.

'I won't say another word,' she said, extending her hand by way of recompense. Furtively he took it.

What was that woman thinking? Aren't they a charming couple? Or perhaps, where are they going together at this time of year? With only one suitcase too. Steven withdrew his hand.

'I never went to the seaside for a holiday,' he said sadly.

But there had been a time hadn't there? George had taken him out to Eastbourne one Sunday when he'd been at prep school. They had hired a rowing-boat. As the beach got further away the noise of the people talking grew vaguer, a dull roar extending for miles, like a monstrous cocktail party. It was very hot he remembered. When they were about a mile out George had decided to go for a swim. He'd swum a long way, almost out of sight. Or had the distance seemed further then? He had panicked. What would happen if George didn't come back? He'd heard the murmur from the beach going on indifferently. He'd never be able to row all that distance to the beach. And nobody would hear if he called. 'George, George,' he'd yelled.

And if after tomorrow his mother rejected him? If David wouldn't say anything? If George survived? What then? 'If you made as many friends as you made enemies, you'd be a popular man,' Robert had once said. Steven grinned. All very fine, but when it came to it, when one really had nobody to call for? Perhaps marriage was the answer. Even if tomorrow was a disaster, she'd never desert him.

He reached out his hand and clasped hers. The woman opposite might not have existed any more. A great welling feeling of tenderness surged within him. He clutched her small hand still tighter.

'Steven you're hurting me.'

Steven let go. If only one could convey one's feelings better. It was stupid to think that one's exact feelings should be reciprocated. He sighed; nevertheless he no longer felt so vulnerable.

❧

George was standing by the drawing-room window, in one hand he was holding Steven's letter and in the other a glass of whisky. He flapped the letter up and down as he spoke.

'Trust him to choose today, of all days to come down here, and as if it wouldn't be enough him coming alone, he has to bring his girl, too.'

'It isn't the best possible moment, darling, I admit, but I think you'll agree that it's nice that he should want to bring her to see us so soon after his engagement.'

Ruth had put down the paper she had been reading and got up. She came over to where George was standing and rested on the end of the sofa.

George's exasperation grew. It was really typical of her to have responded to that telephone call like that. Crofts accuses her son of spreading scandalous rumours, then softens the blow by saying that David is too sensitive for the school, and what does she do? Says that she knew all along that he wasn't happy there and that he'd be happier at the local grammar school. How would he be able to go on living in the same house day in and day out with the living embodiment of his conscience? The very thought of it ...

imagine it, backgammon every evening, looking into those dark accusing eyes. And all the time the fear that David would lose his temper with him and blurt it all out to her. Hadn't the woman any pride? Or was she just going to sit back and take that man's accusation?

'You realise that if you take him away you'll be affirming Crofts's judgement? Have you no pride?' George said, his voice trembling with righteous anger.

'But George dear, David's happiness is more important than my pride.' She leant forward earnestly, her hands clasped in her lap.

'I think that David himself should be allowed to decide.'

George estimated that he would have at least half an hour alone with David in the car, when he collected him from the station. Steven would just *have* to choose David's half-term to come down. If Steven was behaving true to form this could hardly be a coincidence either. The jackals are on the march and it's clearly my blood they're after, he thought grimly. No bicycle made for two was going to be good enough for this wedding. There would have to be a sacrifice too and an unhealthy redistribution of money. He would have to be alone with David and he wouldn't drive fast either. Dimly he heard Ruth's voice:

'Oughtn't we to be going to the station? We don't want to be late.'

'I thought you said you were going to supervise lunch. There are going to be five of us.'

'Hardly an army, darling.' She paused; 'I was thinking of what you said just then about David deciding what was best for him. George, don't you think that he'd be afraid to say what he really felt? He knows that you'd think it was cowardly to back down and I'm sure that he'd hate to disappoint you.'

'And cowardly it is too. I merely think that it would be dictatorial to act without at least asking him his opinion.'

Ruth got up smiling; she slipped an arm round George's waist. Looking up at him lovingly, she said:

'You're so terribly English in your belief in "fair play", but think of all the awful mistakes you would have made if you hadn't been advised when you were young. Anyway, come on, darling, or we really will be late.'

Just another jolly jaunt for her, thought George bitterly, as he walked towards the door and the waiting hearse. The innocent only rarely suffer and all the sinners round them live in an endless nightmare trying to cushion and protect them. To be innocent and a gold-laying goose must surely be the best passport to heaven on earth, thought George sadly.

'Come on, George,' shouted Ruth from the doorway.

Steven paid the taxi-driver and then opened Sarah's door. He held her hand as she stepped out on to the gravel of the drive. She stood quite still looking at the long battlemented front of Trelawn. She turned to Steven wide-eyed.

'You never told me it was so large.'

'We only live in a few rooms; the rest is falling to bits. Mummy had the roof redone last year and it cost £5,000. We can't afford to do-up the inside throughout.'

Steven looked around for George's car but saw it was not there.

'They're collecting David from the station,' he said, as they started towards the door. 'They might have left a bit earlier and saved me twenty-five shillings.'

Suddenly Steven ran in front of Sarah and flung open the doors. 'A warm welcome home to the young mistress,' he croaked, bowing obsequiously.

In the dark hall he took her coat and led her towards the drawing-room.

'What'll you drink before they arrive?'

'Gin and bitter lemon, please.' She gazed through the broad bay-window out across the lawn and beyond that to a group of beeches. Behind the delicate vein tracery of the swaying naked branches dark clouds moved across a grey sky. She heard the tinkling of glass as Steven poured her drink.

'I like this room,' she said, taking the proffered glass.

'Yes.'

'When was the house built?'

'At the end of the last century by a mad wine merchant. Not only did he build the place on top of a hill but he also saw fit that it should face north.'

'Can I see some other bits of the house while the others aren't here.'

'If you like. I'm afraid we don't have a guide.' He paused. 'I think we'll start with my old nursery, so that you can see where I spent so many happy hours.'

Sarah frowned at him.

'If you don't want to show me, I don't mind.'

'Come on. I can't wait.'

The nursery was a large room with whitewashed walls and faded blue linoleum on the floor. It smelt fusty and unaired. All the furniture was under dust sheets. A picture of David hung over the mantelpiece.

'That's your brother?'

'Yes.'

'He's not a bit like you, is he? Much darker.'

'Yes.'

Steven opened a cupboard and looked in at the haphazardly stacked toys. He tried to connect himself with them but couldn't. A train made of large wooden blocks, a number of rusty clockwork boats, a plastic battleship that he had made, several mutilated woolly toys—Steven held one of them up:

'You can see the holes where we used to fire air-gun pellets at him.'

'Lovely.'

Steven's eye lighted on a large metal humming-top. He pulled it out and, setting it on the floor, pressed down the handle. As it spun round and round the thing emitted a low moaning sound. The colours on its side and top merged as they watched.

'That's rather pretty, Steven.'

'Yes. I can't remember liking it as a child.'

The moaning grew softer as it slowed down and finally teetered on to its side noisily under the table.

'So you're Sarah!' Steven watched his mother's smile as she crossed the room. She put her arms around the girl and then stepped back to look at her. Sarah was blushing. 'You don't mind my being awfully continental, dear, do you?'

'Oh no, not at all,' Sarah stammered.

'They all shake hands on the Continent,' said George coldly.

'In Italy too?' Ruth laughed. Nobody was going to pour cold water on this family-gathering for her.

'This is my brother, David,' said Steven, leading a reluctant David over to where Sarah was standing. 'David, this is Sarah. She saw your portrait in the nursery and doesn't think we're alike. I'm more like my father I'm told.' Steven smiled at George, who looked away. David's introductory smile had faded. Uneasily he studied his feet.

'Steven tells me you're home for your half-term,' Sarah said helpfully.

David nodded. If the conversation in the car had been anything to go by, he might be home a little longer than that.

'I expect you're pleased to be home,' she added. What did one say to boys of fifteen?

'Yes, it makes a very nice change,' replied David politely.

'Oh, but darling, you know you love coming home,' Ruth chimed in. 'Besides, you'll be able to play with your beloved train this afternoon.' Ruth's laughter sounded loudly in the silence. David blushed more than ever.

George emptied his glass and started towards the door.

'I think I'll deal with the wine now,' he said.

'Good, darling,' Ruth said. Then to Sarah: 'He's promised us something very special today in your honour.'

'Oh, but it's quite unnecessary. I'm simply hopeless about wine.'

'Oh, are you, dear?'

'Really, I didn't mean that...'

'I know just what you meant, dear.' Ruth inclined her head to one side and smiled again.

So it's to be the great society woman, thought Steven tolerantly; he nodded to Sarah and said to his mother:

'I think I'll go and see if George wants a hand.'

❧

In the dining-room, George was sitting staring vacantly at the three opened wine bottles. Suddenly he was aware of Steven.

'Not feeling well, George, old man?'

'No, just having a bit of peace and quiet while I can.'

'She's not that bad is she? Actually I thought you might quite fancy her yourself. Or aren't the younger ones in your line?' George caught the hardness in Steven's voice. Using the edge of the table to assist him, he rose slowly.

'What do you expect me to say?' he said wearily.

'I hardly expect the truth.'

'If you've come for what I think you have, I suggest you leave well alone.'

'I adore your half-frankness. And what do you suppose I've come for?'

'Well, you'll have a full house anyway. I'm sure your girl-friend is going to like the show.'

'My fiancée, George.'

'Sorry.'

❧

'Now, now, you crusty old men, what are you nattering about that we can't share?' Ruth flowed into the room, drawing Sarah and David behind her.

'Nothing, dear ... Now where are you going to put us all?'

'I thought David could sit next to me and of course Steven and Sarah must sit together on one side. I'm afraid we can't be girl, boy, girl, boy all the way round. But still if Sarah sits between Steven and George...'

'I'll be a hermaphrodite,' said Steven accommodatingly.

It was the middle of the afternoon. Sarah had been found a pair of wellington boots and was being shown round the garden by Ruth. She stopped in front of a small flower-bed.

'This one used to be done entirely by Steven and David. David used to be the keener gardener. I remember we used to take him down plants for his little garden plot at school.'

Sarah moved from one foot to the other. The wellingtons were at least two sizes too small. Still, complaining was out of the question, there'd be all that awful business again about Londoners always coming in flimsy little shoes.

'Would you like to see the rose garden now?'

'Is it far?' said Sarah apprehensively.

'You Londoners...' said Ruth twinkling. 'It'll take us ten minutes I expect.' She pointed over towards a distant group of rhododendrons. Sarah sighed as she vainly tried to emulate Ruth's long strides.

In the drawing-room George was eyeing the whisky bottle. He looked at his watch ... only half past three. Only a small one just to steady the nerves. The newspapers were no good; they just reminded him of the hostile world outside. Glass in hand, he aimlessly walked up and down. Steven was probably with David, but what possible reason could he have for joining them? If he hadn't said anything by now there was a chance that Steven would fail in his persuasion. George went over to the window and looked at the sky. If only I believed in God, he thought.

Steven paused for a moment before knocking on David's door. Inside he could hear the whirring sound of a train on the rails. Hearing no answer he opened the door.

David was lying flat on his stomach peering up the track at the on-coming engine.

'Oh, hello, it's you,' he said, jerking into a crouching position.

'It's grown since I last saw it.'

'I got a lot of new rails at Christmas.'

Steven tried to think when he had last been in his brother's room. He looked at the mass of sidings and junctions sprawling across the floor. Obviously boredom and loneliness was responsible. Or was it all an excuse to be alone?

David watched him staring.

'I suppose you're thinking, like Mummy, that I'm too old to play around with trains.'

'No.'

Steven walked over to the window and drew the curtains. He turned and said:

'I suggest you get up and sit down somewhere comfortable. I want to talk to you.'

'I can hear from here, thank you,' he crossed his legs and squatted in the middle of the central circle of track.

'George thinks he knows why I've come down today. Have you any idea?'

Steven saw that David's face had tensed.

'I expect you'll tell me.'

Already he seemed hostile. Steven wished that he had played with him more when they had been younger. But the age gap had been too much. Five years is a long time to catch up.

'I want to know what you found when you went to George's flat.'

David's voice was shaking with anger:

'So you did plan it, so George was right.'

'I had to. Can't you understand what George is doing to her?'

'Making her happy.'

Steven listened to the humming of the transformer in the otherwise silent room. Slowly he said:

'And when the money's gone will she still be so happy? How much do you suppose that flat in London costs?'

'A lot I expect,' replied David softly.

'Quite right, and how much do you suppose he pays his woman?'

'What woman?' David was relieved that his voice remained firm.

'The woman you found,' said Steven patiently.

'Do you think I wouldn't have told you if I'd found anybody?'

Steven felt his anger growing. With an effort he controlled his temper. That hideous simpering voice: 'Did you think I wouldn't have told you ...' Steven said:

'Obviously you *wouldn't*. But you can't deceive me.' He paused, then snapped: 'Why did you accuse me of "planning it"? Those were your words. Planning what?'

David hesitated before saying:

'Planning getting me into trouble with George. He wasn't pleased to see me, as you said he would be.'

'Why? Why?'

'Because he likes to be alone sometimes. I've got my trains, you can go back to Oxford and George can go to his flat.'

'I have better things to do with my time than "getting you into trouble with George", surprising though that may seem.'

David didn't answer, but got up and went over to the transformer. He flicked the control lever to full speed. He next started to rummage about in a large cardboard box behind him. At last he produced a small goods engine and put it on the inner circle of track. He plugged another smaller transformer into the main one and made a connection with the inner track. Soon both engines were moving round in opposite directions on their different tracks.

As Steven watched, tremors of anger ran through his body. He contracted the muscles in his chest. The sound of the trains maddened him.

'Why don't you put on some carriages too?' he choked.

'Don't be so impatient. I'm going to.'

Something seemed to snap in Steven's chest.

'You bloody little fool,' he yelled as he hurled himself at David. As he hit the ground his foot caught in the goods train; savagely he lashed out with his heel, sending it crashing into one of the table legs. David tried to drag himself clear of the layout, but Steven pulled him back again. They rolled over several times, ripping rails apart and buckling others. David lashed out with his fist and caught Steven just below the ear. Momentarily he let go. David sprang towards the door, but Steven grabbed one of his legs. After several minutes struggling Steven was able to pinion David to the floor. With all his weight across his chest Steven started to twist David's left wrist.

David's breath was coming in sobs as Steven went on twisting.

'What did you find, you little hero, what did you find?' he hissed.

'I told you ... nothing ... nothing.'

Steven twisted one last time.

'Nothing,' yelled David as the tears started.

Steven let go and got up. David stayed sobbing on the floor in the midst of his shattered train set.

Steven looked down at him and said calmly:

'If you won't tell her what you saw, I will. I'll tell her this evening and if you don't back me up, I will never speak to you again so long as I live.'

He turned and walked to the door. When he had opened it he looked back for a moment at his brother's crumpled figure on the floor and said:

'Do it for her.'

Softly he closed the door.

On the stairs he met George.

'I suppose you know, she's going to take him away from Edgecombe?'

Steven walked on down the stairs. From a window on the first landing he saw his mother and Sarah walking towards the house in the growing darkness.

The coffee cups had been cleared away. George was sitting in his wing-chair; he watched Ruth, David and Sarah, on the other side of the room, bent over a game of Scrabble.

'Jolly good, dear. You may even beat our reigning champion, David, if you go on like this. However many does she get for that, darling?' Ruth asked David.

George wondered where Steven had got to. He moved uneasily in his chair. Steven really had thought of everything this time. He had cornered David during the afternoon and now his girl made it impossible for him to talk either to Ruth or David. What in the name of the prophet could Steven have said to the boy? He had knocked on David's door after he had seen Steven going down the stairs, but had got no answer. The door had been locked.

'Well done, David. You've got rid of your "Q" and on a triple word, too.' Ruth herself was trailing. 'Anyway, darling, you'll give her a good run for her money.'

George looked at the little group again. My jury, he thought. Everything depended on their reactions. Nothing could be certain even now. They might decide on the right thing for the wrong reasons or the wrong thing for the right reasons, even on the wrong thing for the wrong reasons. He felt more alert than usual and had not drunk more than a single glass of wine at dinner. He looked round the room, lovingly caressing each ornament with a glance. Even if I was blind, he thought, I could replace them all just by touch. What right had Steven or anybody else to try and alter what time had done? Hadn't he and Ruth bought the glass candlesticks on the mantelpiece? Yes, and the table in the window alcove? From a small junk shop near the harbour in Lymington. It had been sunny and they'd had trouble fitting it into the car. She had given him a handkerchief to mop his brow. 'You're sweating like a pig, darling.' Even the name of the place came back. 'Braggs'. That was it, with two 'gs'. Nothing could change that. Nothing could change the names in the numerous books in the large case in the hall. George heard the door opening and looked up to see Steven coming into the room.

Steven walked over to the mantelpiece and rested an elbow on the shelf.

'Shall we try a game everyone can play?'

'But we haven't finished this one yet. And Sarah's doing awfully well. You've chosen a very clever girl, dear.' Ruth smiled at him.

'I just thought George looked bored sitting all by himself with nobody taking any notice.'

George noticed that Steven's hand was trembling as it hung down over the edge of the mantelpiece.

'Anyway, George, I've come down especially to play with you. I thought you might care for a little truth game. How about starting then, George?'

'Don't be childish.'

'Oh no, George, you must play, it might be such fun. We used to play when we were children. "My most embarrassing moment," that sort of thing,' Ruth said as she came over to George's chair and sat on the arm. Steven saw Sarah look away as his mother ran her fingers through George's hair. 'Come on, dear,' she laughed playfully. 'My most embarrassing moment.'

'That will do very nicely,' Steven added. 'You must be absolutely truthful. I can assure you that when it's my turn I shall be.'

'I don't doubt that.'

'Well, if George won't start, how about you, David?' Steven stared his brother full in the eyes. David looked away and said nothing. 'No need to be shy. I'm sure that your most embarrassing moment is no worse than George's.'

George said:

'The person who proposes the game ought to start.'

'I'll start then,' said Steven. He saw Sarah looking at him anxiously. David seemed to have found a new significance in his trousers legs. Steven turned to George and began:

'Mine happened this afternoon when I found myself fighting on the floor with my brother. I broke up his train set. Even the new rails and engine he got for Christmas.'

'Don't listen to him,' David broke out. 'It isn't true.'

'Shall we go and look then?' Steven replied coolly.

'I don't think this is very funny, Steven. I think we'd better stop if you're going to behave like this in front of Sarah,' said Ruth.

'She is at perfect liberty to leave the room when she wants to. I can assure you I didn't find it funny either. Nor did David. Did you?'

Everyone was looking at him. David pressed his nails into the palms of his hands and managed to stop himself speaking. The longer he remained silent, the more chance there was that Steven would lose his temper. Sarah saw that he was shaking. She sat on the edge of her chair wishing that she had the courage to get up and leave the room. If only she knew what Steven wanted her to do. This was so unexpected, so horrible.

'Shall I tell them why I nearly bust your wrist then? Or perhaps George would like to suggest a reason?'

'I think this has gone quite far enough,' said George, starting to get up.

'I agree,' added Ruth. 'I expect Sarah's tired and wants to go and unpack and get to bed.'

'I expect Sarah is old enough to look after herself. Do I have to repeat the question or are you determined that I'm going to play alone?'

George sank back into his chair. Why the hell didn't Ruth take her bottom off the arm?

'What would I want to know from David?' asked Steven again.

George saw Steven's face thrust near to his. It was twisted with anger.

'Your behaviour is hardly my responsibility,' he said quietly.

'No, George? Do you suppose that you never affected me? Do you remember how, when you used to come to school plays and concerts, I always made excuses so I didn't have to sit with you? "Is that your father?" "How old was he when he married your mother?" "Fifteen?" Not only that, but you always had to go and have coffee with Crofts too after it was over. "This is my friend, Mr. George Benson." And what do you suppose they said when you had gone? You didn't have to have Crofts's tactfully indirect and searching questions.'

'Did it matter what other people said?' Ruth said with a shaking voice.

'Yes, it did. It mattered a lot. You could go back to your fool's paradise but I had to listen.'

'I didn't think you were so sensitive,' said George.

'So it's a joke is it? I wonder if David still finds it such enormous fun.'

George felt the anger of the righteous boiling within him.

'What do you suppose those visits were like for me?' he asked.

'You didn't have to come.'

'Who'd have driven your mother?'

'You could have worn a peaked cap and sat in the car.'

'Did it ever occur to your twisted little mind that a woman needs a man? Your mother's a woman you know. A very human one too.'

'If you're trying to tell me I've got an Oedipus complex, you're wasting your time. Who was always Mummy's boy, David? If I didn't like it, God knows what it was like for you watching them pinching each other. Did you ever hear anything at night? Your bedroom was next to theirs. Or did you bury your head in the pillow and cover your ears?'

'Leave him alone, can't you?' George hissed. 'It's me you're gunning for, isn't it?'

'Steven, I'm not going to listen to you any more. I'm going straight up to bed. If you think I'm going to go on sitting here listening to such revolting things ... George was almost a father to you both.' Her voice was trembling. Sarah felt sick as she watched the tears start to spill down Ruth's cheeks.

'Almost a father ... yes, taught us what "cads" were before we even went to school. The boy's guide to the old grey stones. Responsible citizenship, the right way by a perfect pillar of society. Look at him ... just look at him.'

The sight of Steven shaking his head from side to side goaded George to his feet. Pushing Ruth aside he leapt up to face Steven. With difficulty he said:

'I made sacrifices too.'

'It must be a real nightmare to have such a lot of free time and free drink. Why, you might have been a provincial bank manager by now.'

'I might and I might have preserved my self-respect.'

'And your liver,' Steven sneered.

Ruth was crying softly, bent double over the arm of the chair.

'Why did you do it for me? George, why did you do it? Why?' she wailed.

'Perhaps David will tell you. Or has he lost his tongue?'

There was a long silence, punctuated by Ruth's sobs.

'Was it for love or money, George?' Steven went on.

'You can't hurt her like this. Steven, you can't,' David whispered unbelievingly.

'Hasn't George ever opened his book of clichés and told you sometimes one has to be cruel to be kind?'

'Get out of here. Get out,' George said weakly, without moving.

'I'll hit you if you touch me,' Steven leered at him. 'Anyway, don't I have some right to part-ownership? You've got a place in London, so there's no need to be selfish.' He watched his mother's body convulse. 'And besides, you even have a nice little woman to look after you.'

'I won't listen. I won't,' Ruth screamed.

'It's lies, all lies,' George said almost to himself. 'He's got no proof. What colour are her eyes, what does she wear?' George paused. 'You can't tell me, can you? You can't tell me because she doesn't exist.'

Ruth clutched at his hand.

'I believe you, darling, I do.'

'Oh no, oh no, oh no,' Sarah groaned with her head buried in the side of the sofa.

'You want to believe it. That's what you mean, isn't it,' Steven shouted. 'But David can tell you that I'm right. Tell them what you saw when you were in London that night, you idiot, you won't get another chance.'

David did not answer. Steven crossed the room and implored:

'Tell her, it isn't for me, it's for her; for God's sake.'

'For love or money,' Steven heard George echo tauntingly.

David looked Steven in the eyes and said quietly: 'I warned you, I told you, I saw nothing, nothing.'

Quite suddenly Steven did not care. He went over to his mother and said softly:

'You'll never believe me, but I didn't do this entirely for myself. When the money goes, you see if he doesn't too.'

George had put his arms round her. Her bosom was still shaking with grief and anger. Her head pressed against George's chest, she whispered:

'I never want to see you again.'

Steven walked to the door and beckoned Sarah.

'We're going now.' He turned to his mother and said: 'I'll go as soon as the taxi comes. I'm going to telephone now.'

As he picked up the receiver, he heard her say to David:

'Come here, darling; it's all been awful, I know, but now everything's going to be all right. You see if Mummy isn't right.'

Only when they were in the taxi did Steven notice that Sarah was crying.

'Why did you have to bring me?'

'I thought I could win,' Steven said simply.

'You were so cruel, so horrible.'

'I was so brave and he was so cowardly. The little coward, the silly little coward.'

Sarah was surprised to see that his expression was not one of scorn but of bewilderment.

'He used to get up at six o'clock in the morning to scare the rabbits away so that we couldn't shoot them, yet he defended that man. He found him in that flat with another woman and he still loves him. I don't understand. I simply don't understand any more.'

He seemed to be talking to himself. Sarah put an arm round him.

'So it was true. It wasn't all for yourself. You didn't bring me just because you wanted money ... Poor Steven.'

'Poor Steven,' he said, burying his face in the fur of her collar.

Part Two: 1965

❧   ❧   ❧

ONE

I T was such a lovely walk to the church through the fields. At the next gate she would be able to look down across the valley and see the simple square tower peeping through a gap in the trees of the woods below. Ruth hurried on eagerly.

She paused at the gate. There was the tower with the sun shining on its lichened walls. She could hear the sound of the bells rising in waves through the morning haze. Quite a long way to go yet. She took off her coat. So warm already . . . it was going to be another marvellous hot day. She breathed in deeply and stretched out her arms.

In a few minutes she was coming down from the corn fields into the woods. The bells were louder now.

George lazed in a deck-chair on the front lawn. He was still in his silk dressing-gown. A large straw hat sheltered him from the rays of the still-climbing sun. Putting down the papers for a moment, he leant out and lifted his glass of iced coffee from the small table beside him. David was away for a couple of days with an old school friend from Edgecombe days. Ruth would be at church for the next hour and a half or so. He gazed across the well-mown lawn towards the herbaceous border. He listened to the enveloping humming of the bees.

At length he got up and walked over to the bench by the sundial, so that he could look back at the house. He looked down at his stomach and beneath it his slippered feet swinging across the grass. Fatter and balder, he thought without emotion. There would have been a time when he cared; but now there was little point. Now there was little to disturb his peace of mind.

There had been one narrow escape. Sally had telephoned shortly after his deliverance from Steven. George had left for London the following day, ostensibly to see his mother. He had calmed himself with the thought that a glance at his bank statement would mark the ending of Sally's infatuation. In the event this had proved unnecessary. He had stayed at the flat for a couple of days awaiting her arrival. Her letter had been short. She hated to have to tell him that there had been others and that, well, an offer, as generous as one that she had just received, should not be idly cast aside. Even after five years George remembered his joy with undiminished pleasure. He'd been a fool to have supposed she just sat at home demurely waiting for his monthly appearances. And a girl like her ... He nodded his head self-critically at the thought of his stupidity. But all that was so long ago. Over and done with, he reflected. At last the future was as clear as the neatly trimmed hedges in the rose garden. In October David was going to Cambridge and would take with him for the major part of the year the less pleasant features of an earlier landscape. He would make new friends who might ask him to stay; he would go abroad with them. In fact there was every possibility that he would spend little time at Trelawn. Of course there was no need to be uncharitable. The boy had been remarkably little trouble. He'd spent most of his time working in his room. The old twinges of guilt were intermittent almost to the point of non-existence.

The day Steven's old room had been turned into a junk room had been the turning-point. Now his name was hardly ever mentioned.

Ruth had changed for the better too. She was less excitable, and her church-going not only gave her an outside interest but also often kept her occupied during the evenings. She was embroidering hassocks.

When George reached the bench he realised that the sun would be in his eyes if he sat there. Slowly he ambled back to his old chair.

As soon as he sat down he saw a small black car almost half a mile away slowly coming up the drive. It disappeared momentarily behind the group of beech-trees and then emerged in front of the dark-leaved rhododendrons. He wondered whether it might be David coming back earlier than expected. To be caught by anybody else in his dressing-gown at this hour would be annoying. Nobody from the village ever came unless invited. The sun caught on the car's windscreen as it rounded the bend into the final sweep up to the house. George hastily removed his straw hat and drew his dressing-gown more closely round him.

Ruth sat listening to the First Lesson. She pursed her lips slightly as Canon Jenner read out:

'... Then was Nebuchadnezzar full of fury, and the form of his visage was changed against Shadrach, Meshach, and Abed-nego...'

Really it was too bad that he should have chosen to read about the 'fiery furnace' on such a lovely day. It was definitely more a winter piece. She would have to talk to him about it afterwards. The hymn before had been a notable contrast though. She smiled at her realisation of the joke... 'From Greenland's icy mountains' to the fiery furnace. Even George would be bound to laugh at that.

'... Did not we cast three men bound into the midst of the fire? They answered and said unto the king, True, O king. He answered and said, Lo, I see four men loose, walking in the midst of the fire, and they have no hurt ...'

Ruth stared up at the patterns on the walls made by the sun shining through the stained glass of the east window. On days like these it was so easy to believe.

George raised his paper in front of him and sat back in his

chair with apparent unconcern. No reason to be put out by uninvited visitors. He did not look up as he heard the muted sound of footsteps on the grass, and the faint swish of a dress.

'George?' questioned a voice on the other side of the newspaper.

He lowered his defence and saw a woman wearing a tight-fitting coat and skirt in front of him. Must have been the lilac coat on her arm that he had heard. Her eyes were hidden behind a large pair of dark glasses.

'I don't think we've met.'

'Not for five years anyway, George. Remember now?' She jerked off her dark glasses and smiled at him.

George felt sick. The green lawn might have been a sea of corpses, the sun a monstrous skull for all they pleasure they promised now.

'Sally,' he groaned.

It was ten minutes later; they were in the drawing-room. George was fumbling around over by the writing-desk. If only he could find it. A consecutive run of bank statements ought to be enough to convince her that she had wasted her time. They used to be in a large buff-coloured envelope. Damn the weather for being so hot. He felt the sweat trickling down his back.

'What are you up to over there?' he heard her ask.

'I'm just trying to prove to you that I've got no money. That I lied to you, that I'm nothing more than a blood-sucking parasite.'

'What makes you so sure that I've come for money?' she asked pleasantly.

'You'd hardly have made the journey for old time's sake on a stifling day like this.'

'I haven't come for your money, George, I've come for you.'

'Look, you simply don't understand ... I can't leave ... I've got responsibilities,' he ended lamely.

'Anyway you can't fool me about the money. You don't suppose I'm going to believe that she paid for that flat of yours?'

George went on looking, even when he knew that he was not going to find the envelope. He turned round and saw that she had brought his straw hat in from the garden.

'I'd never thought of you wearing funny hats here. More hunting-clothes and dinner-jackets was how I imagined it.' She held out the hat towards him. 'Won't you put it on?'

'No, I won't.'

'Be like that then.' She laughed loudly.

'I'm afraid you're going to have to go now,' he said firmly. 'You had your chance, but you turned me down. I suppose you've forgotten that. I'm not going to let myself in for that sort of thing again.' He looked at her with more confidence. Should have taken the firm line earlier on.

'If it comes to forgetting, I don't suppose you remember what you promised. It's all square now. A perfect basis for further negotiations. Being a soldier I expect you know all about that.' She smiled.

'It takes two to come to an agreement,' said George with decision. 'It's too late now.'

'Five years isn't a lifetime you know. I'm prepared to forgive you for shutting me out in the snow. After all, you started the distrust. You can't blame me for taking revenge. But I've realised now that I was wrong. I'm not going to make the same mistake again. I was silly, but I've learned a bit since then.'

'I don't doubt it. How many has it been? How do I know there haven't been five or six? So you've been chucked out once too often and have come crawling here. Well, you can crawl straight out again.'

'Not crawling, George. I've come back to the only person who ever mattered.'

'You've taken your time about it. Why did the last one throw you out? Or should I ask why did he ever have you in the first place? Five years may not be a lifetime but twenty years is a good deal closer. I've been with her too long to just get up and leave. There comes a time when it really is too late.'

'Would it still be too late if I decided to stay for a few hours more?'

George looked at her with disgust.

'You've got too much make-up on your eyes,' he said.

'Maybe because I haven't had you to keep me young and chaste.'

She seemed fatter now; he noticed the curving creases in her skirt just below the stomach. There was a hint of too much flesh beneath the jaw.

'There's another train at twelve-twenty. I'll drive you there.'

'You'll be driving a bit further. And, what's more you'll be taking me too. It's going to be just the two of us now. She's had her go, now it's my turn.' She stood legs apart with her hands on her hips.

'If you told Ruth, she wouldn't believe you. You'd better come now. Steven told her and she didn't believe him and he's a lot cleverer than you and knew her rather better.'

'You don't suppose she'd believe me if I told her the dates you went to see your mother? Or would it be more convincing if I threw in a description of her son as well?'

George watched her as she paced up and down in front of the sunlit window. The incongruity of her presence made him dry up inside. What did she understand about beautiful things? About the table that he and Ruth had bought, about real candles that one lit? About art and poetry? George tried to think of some of the beautiful lines he knew by heart, but couldn't. How could she ever understand the tranquillity of life in the country: the simple round of rural pleasures? She probably didn't even like the room they were in. To have survived so long and then to lose all this for a little slattern would be too hard to endure.

Sally coughed loudly. George looked at his watch. The Second Lesson would have just started and she would be staying for Communion after the Sermon. He said:

'I don't suppose that she would be so impressed if you described David. There's a photograph over there.' He pointed to a silver-framed photograph on a small table by the door. 'She would think you just met me in a pub and saw my address on a letter to me and thought that you'd try a bit of cheap blackmail.'

'She wouldn't be impressed if I told her the date David was in London? You say Steven told her. If I told her the same tale you still think that she wouldn't smell a rat?'

'She doesn't remember dates. She'd think you were making them up.'

Or did she? George thought of her diary. If he could get his hands on it ... he rushed across to the writing-desk. She kept it in the top drawer. He pulled. It was locked. Could probably break it open. He wrenched again but it wouldn't give.

'I should think that's quite an expensive piece of furniture; it would be a pity to spoil it.'

Of course the thing mightn't be there anyway. There wasn't time to search the house. Only one thing to be done. He'd have to go with her now. Make her believe that he was going for good. Pack a few cases and get out. He could phone Ruth and tell her that his mother had been suddenly taken ill. He could leave a note. Better still. If it was money she was after, his mother could be made to have an operation in a private hospital. Ruth would be sure to send a cheque.

While they were packing, George looked at his watch. Ruth might be back in twenty minutes. Hastily he pulled down two large suitcases from the top of his wardrobe. To convince Sally it would be necessary to take a lot of clothes. He dropped several pairs of shoes into the bottom of one of the cases and then ripped a couple of suits off their hangers before thrusting them in too.

Sally said:

'How about some shirts?'

They were all in the chest of drawers in the bedroom. Perfect, this was the chance to leave a note.

'Won't be a moment.'

In the bedroom, George tore the fly-leaf out of a book on the bedside table and wrote: 'Mother sinking. Operation imminent. Sorry mess. Will ring you. George.' He read it through and hastily inserted 'All love'. It would save time if he took the whole drawer to the dressing-room. He lifted it out.

❧

When he got back Sally was thrusting a pair of pyjamas into the second case. He looked down and saw his bedroom slippers. No time to change. He pulled some trousers on top of his pyjama bottoms and then jerking off his dressing-gown he reached for a jersey and slipped it on. He snatched the jacket, he had worn the day before, from the back of a chair.

Sally sat on the suitcases while he fastened them up. She was as eager as he to get away before Ruth arrived. A last final appeal and generous offers of forgiveness were highly undesirable.

❧

George led the way down the stairs. The cases thudded against the banisters. Should have made her go first, he thought uneasily. Still they were nearly at the bottom now. He could hear her behind him.

'I've got to go somewhere before I go,' Sally suddenly announced.

An argument would take too long.

'All right. But hurry.'

❧

Sally ran up to the landing again. George had left the bedroom door open. Softly she stole inside. On the bed the note was where George had left it.

'Cunning bastard,' she said under her breath.

Still holding the note tightly she ran into the lavatory.

George heard the noise of it flushing from the hall. She was certainly being quick.

Sally was not satisfied though. Just like at the pictures, she thought as she dropped a lipstick and a bottle of scent outside the bedroom. Hadn't she read about something like this in some old book?

'Come on,' yelled George from below.

'Ready now.'

As they walked out through the hall door, George looked at his watch again. Definitely no time to check upstairs. Have to get the cases in and turn the car. The distant sound of church bells decided him. The suitcases bumped painfully against his thighs as he ran towards the car.

TWO

R U T H walked slowly across the lawn humming softly. She saw George's chair with the coloured squares of the cushions resting on it. There was his glass of coffee that she had made him. The Sunday papers were lying crumpled on the ground. She smiled; dear George, he was always so untidy. But men always are.

As she went through the front door, she patted her brow with a small handkerchief. So hot ... how lucky that they were going to have salad. In the drawing-room the writing-desk was open. She crossed the room and closed it. What a mess he made; but it was useless trying to change people. One learnt that with age.

❦

'George,' she called. Getting no answer, she started to climb the stairs. He would probably be dressing. She opened the door of their bedroom and let out a small cry. Drawers were open, articles of clothing lay scattered on the floor. She ran out on to the landing and threw open the door of George's dressing-room. There were no cases on top of the wardrobe. She thrust aside the curtains and looked down the drive. The car had gone. She stood there for some moments completely still, apparently incapable of movement. Her body shook violently several times before she let herself slip to the ground. Crumpled in a kneeling position, with her chin resting on the window ledge, her sobbing grew more rapid. At first the spasms hurt but gradually each rhythmic and slowly swelling bubble of grief grew and broke easily from the one before. It was some minutes before she moved.

A sudden glimmer of hope gave her the strength to rise. He might have left a note in the hall.

On the stairs she stumbled and fell. Her foot had hit something hard and round. She saw Sally's lipstick rolling away from her on the landing. Her grief gave way to a feeling of terror. Perhaps one of the cleaners had dropped it. It was then that she saw the bottle of scent.

Ruth gripped the receiver so tightly that her hand began to ache.

'Operator, this is a serious call ... please, please try and do it quickly.'

In a couple of seconds she was speaking to David.

'You must come back. Something awful has happened ... now, now on the next train. I can't be alone...'

'Oh Steven, Steven,' she cried as she let the receiver fall. 'I don't want to wake up tomorrow, I don't.'

In the drawing-room the clock on the mantelpiece struck two.

THREE

STEVEN tipped the contents of his wire basket on to the supermarket cash desk: a packet of frozen fish fingers, some dried peas, a tin of peaches and a packet of mashed potato powder. The girl slipped them into a carrier bag and handed it to him. He pocketed his change and pushed his way out into the street. The warm air was full of the smell of petrol fumes.

Saturday was always murder. He had had a pie and some chips after leaving the office. Now he was on his way to collect Robin from school. Robin was four.

The school was in a small street near Kensington Gardens. From several doors away Steven could hear the high-pitched noise of playing children. The paved garden in front of the house was used as a playground. He opened the gate and went in. A group of children in blazers were jumping up and down on a garden bench. One of them fell off. Steven heard a loud wail of grief as he entered the hall.

'I've come to collect Robin Lifton,' he said to a tall grey-haired woman hurrying towards the sound of the yelling.

'First on the left,' she said, walking on past him. Steven looked after her through the open door. The children were standing back respectfully from their wounded brother, who was lying moaning on the ground.

He turned and went into the classroom indicated. Robin was sitting alone colouring the sea in a large picture of a battleship.

'It should be blue.'

'Miss Lang says it's green and that's how you tell it from the sky.'

In the playground the grey-haired woman came up to Steven and smiled.

'Are you Robin's father?' she asked.

'Yes.'

'I don't believe I've ever had the pleasure ... I'm Miss Lang.'

'The one who thinks the sea is green when the sky is blue?'

'You see the children get so confused with colours,' she twinkled.

'I'm not surprised,' said Steven as he towed Robin towards the gate.

'Mummy's out with Granny this afternoon. So we're going for a walk in the park.'

'Can you buy me a boat to sail on the pond?'

'I can, but I'm not sure if I will.'

'Please, please,' Robin in cap and blazer jumped along beside him chanting, 'Please, Daddy, ple—ase.'

'Perhaps.'

They came out of a toyshop with a plastic clockwork tug. Robin clutched it lovingly. Every few steps he looked at it. Just outside the park gates he walked into an elderly woman. Steven said:

'Look where you're going, or I'll take it away.'

Robin made a great show of looking where he was going.

Steven looked around him disdainfully. The usual crop of week-end cotton frocks spotted the burnt grass. Like litter he thought, just like litter. It had not rained for weeks and the grass and paths looked dirty.

Robin had seen a man with a tray of choc-ices.

'Can I have one, Daddy?'

'No.'

152

'Please, please, Da—a—ddy.'

'Keep quiet or I'll take your boat away.'

Steven lowered the tug into the water.

'Are you sure you wound it up enough to get it to make a circle?'

'Yes, yes, let it go, let it go.'

Robin was hopping on one leg with excitement. The small boat progressed jerkily a few feet from the edge and stopped before turning back.

'I thought you said you wound it up enough.'

'I did. Perhaps you didn't hold it right.'

'Well, I'm not going to wait all day for it to come back. The wind isn't helping us for a start.'

Robin began to cry.

'You're not still a baby. What do you suppose the other children will think?'

'I don't care. I want my boat back.'

'I'll get another.'

'I don't want another.'

Robin was standing right on the edge, craning his neck forwards to try and be closer to his boat. Suddenly he slipped.

'Haven't you ever been told not to stand so near the edge?'

Steven looked at him. He was wet to the waist. Robin was crying again.

'We were going to listen to the band, but now we can't.'

The crying grew more plaintive. What a bore to have to take him home so early. Perhaps as it was so hot the trousers could dry on him.

'All right, we'll stay.'

'Will you get me another boat, Daddy?'

'Not today.'

'Can we listen to the band now?'

'Yes. I want you to sit very quietly.'

On the way to the bandstand another child threw a ball that bounced a few feet in front of Robin. He picked it up and hurled it clumsily. It hit a man lying full length on the ground.

'Go and say you're sorry.'

Robin clung to Steven's leg and buried his face in the folds of his jacket.

'Didn't you hear me?'

The man said:

'Really, it doesn't matter.'

'I think it does. Robin, go and say you're sorry.'

Robin broke away from him and started to run off through the mass of human refuse. Steven stared angrily after him.

In the distance he could hear the band playing 'Colonel Bogey'.

❧

Sarah was sitting watching the television when they got home. She looked up as they came into the room.

'Did you remember the cooking-oil?'

'No.'

'We can't have any dinner then.'

'You can do it in butter.'

'You know how much that costs.'

Steven went over and switched off the television.

'Don't ask me, will you?'

'No.'

Robin had picked up a belt that had been lying on the table and was swishing it about. He knocked over a vase of flowers.

'Out,' shouted Steven. 'Out.'

'If you'd watched him instead of fiddling about with the television, he wouldn't have done that.'

'I have been watching him all the bloody afternoon. I could have thought that you might have a try now.'

'Who'll be watching him every day of the next holidays?'

'Who'll be working every day of the next holidays?'

Steven looked at her with contempt. He was very conscious of the shape of her skull under her hair. There were bags under her eyes and she hadn't bothered to make-up.

'I'm always so tired these days,' she said. 'Daddy thinks I need a holiday.'

'Fine, if he pays for it.'

'If you earned a bit more . . .'

'I've told you a thousand times that this job is mainly to gain experience. I don't enjoy it any more than you do.'

'You don't seem in any hurry to change it.'

'Would you like filing items in a vast card-index system and then making checks on sales and stock? Not only that, but I do the accounts as well.'

'You'd think they'd pay you more for all that.'

Robin came back into the room and picked up the vase. He put it carefully on its side on the table. Any water that had not gone on the carpet went on the table. Neither of them took any notice.

'If you'll only look forward a bit, instead of always carping, you'd realise the value of what I'm doing.'

'That's what you said with the last job.'

'That was different.'

'I hope so.'

Robin walked over to his mother and put his head on her knee.

'My trousers are wet, Mummy.'

'He fell in the pond,' supplied Steven.

'You didn't bring him home at once?'

'What the hell does it look like? We listened to the band.'

'You couldn't be bothered; isn't that it?'

'It was hot enough to fry an egg in the park.'

'If he catches a cold . . .'

'I've had enough. I'm going out to supper.'

'Daddy's a silly old crossy,' whined Robin.

'If you repeat anything your mother says to me, I'll hit you.'

Robin cowered nearer Sarah. Steven slammed the door behind him.

'Every blasted day of the week,' he muttered as he started down the badly lit stairs.

FOUR

THE number 30 carried George through the relentless rain along the Old Brompton Road and then into Lillie Road. His eyes passed over the broad expanse of Brompton Cemetery. Into drabber and less-ordered Fulham the bus drove inexorably on, towards a land of commons, filter beds and reservoirs.

Going home to beg at my age is degradation indeed, he thought. He looked out gloomily at the rows of sooty and crumbling houses. No more the pleasures of England's pastures green for him. Only the dark and dank embrace of the satanic mills remained.

'Putney High Street,' he said to the conductor. His change felt wet and sticky. In front of him a group of schoolgirls in plum-coloured blazers were chattering excitedly. George looked at them without emotion. They were probably going home too.

The bus was turning into Fulham Palace Road. Yet another cemetery. The place was full of them.

George's mind once again slipped back over the events of the last two days. There had been compensations: Sally's expression, after she had seen his London bank manager and his former stockbroker, had offered momentary solace. She had, however, created the most distasteful scene in the street which quite spoiled his brief enjoyment of her face. Delicately he ran his hand over his left temple where she had struck him with her umbrella handle. She had also called him a number of things which he had so far not managed to forget. The single night he had spent at her flat was to be his last. His two suitcases were now in the Left Luggage at Earls Court station. He managed a fairly convincing imitation of a smile as he thought of the affection she had lavished on him immediately before her disillusionment.

Still rubbing his wounded temple, he had asked her why she was not going to try and make him get some money out of Ruth. She had told him about the scent and the lipstick.

Putney Bridge already. He stared out across the yards and yards of rain-spattered mud. The tide always seemed to be out when he went home.

His telephone call to Ruth had been, he reflected, painful, expensive, and unnecessary. She had obviously had the real story out of David as well has having found Sally's relics.

His mother might be able to let him have ten pounds but little more. The only thing Ruth did not own was the car. He had put an advertisement in the evening papers. With luck it might raise £100.

The water dripped down the neck of his macintosh as he walked down the street where his mother had lived since his father's death over twenty years before. The pavement glistened underfoot and the drains bubbled vociferously. At last he was standing outside the familiar green door.

'Well, this is a pleasant surprise. I thought you'd quite given up your old mother.' She looked at her son standing in the rain. His hair was plastered down over his forehead. 'Come on in then, and I'll get you some nice hot tea.'

George followed her into the sitting-room. Pictures of a more youthful George reproached him from every side. She saw the direction of his glances.

'You used to be a sweet little boy,' his mother said nostalgically.

Staffordshire figures crowded each other to death on the mantelpiece. The owl in its glass case still stared out through dried ferns and varnished leaves. In the windows heavy net curtains shut out most of the light of an already grey day.

'Can we have a light on?' George asked.

'I wonder if you could dust the shade before you go? I can't get up on chairs like I used to.'

George nodded. His mother went out to get the tea.

She came into the room again bowed with the weight of her tray. George recognised the solid willow-pattern cups that had been used since his childhood.

'Can I help you?' he said, getting up.

She put down the tray and started pouring without answering. She at least didn't seem to have changed a great deal. Still small, grey-haired and slightly stooping. Her eyes were perhaps a shade less bright, her nose a fraction sharper.

'You don't come and see me as often as you used,' she said without bitterness.

'Well, I'm here now,' he said jovially.

'You've got your own life to lead. I'm not complaining.'

She held out a plate of assorted biscuits. George picked one out and nibbled delicately. It was rather dry. His mother said:

'I was never happy when you went off with that woman. But it's your life.' She took a sip of tea and then resumed. 'You make your bed and lie on it. It's up to you to make what you will of it. I only hope that you're still doing that job at the quarry.'

George nodded feebly. It was going to be impossible to break it to her. Was it his shame or a feeling of genuine pity for her? George hoped it was pride and the remnants of his self-respect. He had told that lie about the quarry years ago so that she could still be proud of him. In those days he had usually arrived in a large chauffeur-driven car, which he hired from a near-by garage. 'Come up for a business meeting; we're opening another quarry. So I thought I'd combine business with pleasure.' He heard his former voice with disgust. There was an extra bedroom upstairs but obviously he couldn't tell her the truth.

'Yes, I'm still managing the quarry,' he said at last.

His mother looked at him dubiously.

'We're not doing so well these days,' he added quickly.

'You must go on all the same,' she said sharply. The old glint was in her eyes again for a moment. 'Your father, bless him, always used to say that a kept man is no man.'

'I remember him saying that.'

'Of course he didn't like it any more than I did when you went away like that. Still, if you fly in the face of society you take your life in your hands and if you fail, you pay the consequences. If, though, you can stand and say to society: "I'm quite happy, thank you very much indeed," well and good.'

'That's how I look at it,' said George.

His mother went on chewing at a biscuit. George looked at the picture behind her chair: a meticulously painted Highland scene.

'I remembered it as having a stag in the foreground,' said George.

'There isn't one.'

'No, there isn't, is there.'

His mother went on chewing with greater determination. She said:

'You were never very keen on pictures when you were little. You preferred soldiers.' She paused and said more softly: 'When I look at the lake in that painting I long to swim in it. I've never been to Scotland.'

George said nothing. Although it was summer it seemed nearly dark outside. The hiss of the rain went on unabated. The room looked much cosier now. The heavily shaded lamps glowed warmly. He thought of the wet streets. The upstairs bedroom had become unbearably attractive. He opened his mouth to speak but no sound came. With an effort he got up.

'I'm afraid I've got to go now.'

'So soon? I don't see you very often but I suppose when there are people waiting one has to go.'

She was lonely and really wanted him to stay. The bedroom tempted him once more. He held his head higher, resigned at last.

'Good-bye then, Mummy.'

He felt like crying as he embraced her. Never had he known the same longing to be at home.

His hair had dried inside the house. He felt the rain beginning to weight it down. Not long till it would be dribbling down his collar again. He walked on quickly. Near the end of the street he stooped to look at his reflection in a car window. He would hardly qualify for the Y.M.C.A. The Salvation Army might be a better bet.

When he reached the final corner of his mother's street he realised that he had forgotten to ask for any money. He looked back for a moment and then started to run in the opposite direction. The five pounds he still had might last till the sale of the car.

He paused on Putney Bridge and looked down at the dark water. Not to be thought of ... there was every possibility that he would scream and be rescued. That would only make matters worse.

His feet moved under him. He would catch the tube somewhere. He would at least be dry while he was in the thing. He stared hard at his feet as he walked on. His shoes were so well polished, his trouser creases so neatly pressed. 'Pathetic, that's what it is, pathetic!' He raised a hand to his eyes. Pure waste of time. In this weather it was impossible to tell tears from rain. George smarted under the increasing downpour. Each drop seemed a personal insult. And yet each drop also seemed a challenge.

FIVE

RUTH looked at her bank manager's letter yet again, as though to convince herself of its reality. The point for no longer ignoring these communications had clearly been reached. She was informed that she now had insufficient money in shares to clear her overdraft. It would have to be the house next. She would have to sell beloved Trelawn where they had all once been so happy. Soon the so-familiar rooms would be bare, and alien feet would sound loudly on the uncarpeted boards. Out of their present context how could any of the pictures or ornaments have any significance? How much one took for granted. How easy it was to look around one without ever really seeing. Why, she had never noticed till now the delicate patterning on the metal plates just above and below the door-handles. Had she ever thought of the light-switches as being made of brass and as jutting out from the wall? But didn't a place become home when one no longer saw small details but rather understood everything only in relation to the general picture?

She heard the drawing-room door opening and turned to see David coming into the room. He had grown so tall and handsome in the last couple of years. He at least would never desert her. He would have to know the truth. There was no time left for concealment now.

'We're going to have to sell Trelawn,' she said softly. The idea seemed more possible now that she had spoken it.

'Where will we go instead?' The 'we' had come almost automatically, David noticed. It was so much easier to avoid mentioning inevitable ruptures. Hadn't he been doing that ever since George's departure two weeks ago? Of course he would stay with her. He had done the same in answering her letters when he had been at school. Anything to avoid present trouble.

'We'll find a nice little flat in London. You'll be able to bring home your new friends from Cambridge. There'll be lots of parties in London too,' she said smiling at him.

David knew how much she hated London. He saw the added blackmail only too well, but still he could not bring himself to say anything.

'You'd like that, wouldn't you, darling?'

'Yes, I'd like that.' So much easier, thought David. After all when he had betrayed Steven he had entirely committed himself should George ever betray him.

His mother had evidently been thinking of Steven too. She said nostalgically:

'I want so much to bury the past. After what has happened it's only right that we should see Steven again. You know how I suffered, how much he has been on my mind. I want you to go and see him in London. You could go in a couple of days. I know you'll do it, darling. Somehow I feel it will come better from you.'

'Perhaps it would.'

'Oh, darling...' She got up, and came across the room towards him with open arms. Clasping him tightly, she whispered:

'Darling, it's only for you that I go on living.'

SIX

THE brand in the cave man's hand lit and the sky in the mouth of the cave darkened. Robin pressed the button again and night once more replaced day in a second.

It was another Saturday and Sarah was seeing her mother again. Three weeks ago it had been the Natural History Museum. This time the sciences were under scrutiny.

Steven watched Robin progressing from case to case, pressing the buttons as he went. 'Lighting through the Ages': the wall-brackets glowed and now it was the turn of a group of centurions to see the sudden coming of darkness. Elizabethans blinked as their candles flickered and died, the chandelier in the urban gentility of an eighteenth-century drawing-room lit the keys for a piano player before the light flooded from the tall windows again. The last case showed a pre-war drawing-room with a man and woman sitting in armchairs in front of an electric fire. How many children had gazed at that immutable domestic scene since the thirties? Steven shrugged his shoulders and followed Robin on to an exhibit with weights and pulleys.

'Are you strong enough to lift this one?' asked Robin tugging without success.

Steven pulled the rope and the weight shot up.

'Will I be strong like you, Daddy?'

'I expect so.'

'Will I be strong as an elephant?'

'I don't know.'

They looked into a life-size replica of a medieval blacksmith's shop. Robin saw two men bending over an anvil and heard the hiss of the molten metal. Steven saw three other children trying to push their way closer for a look. The dummies were badly made and looked stiff and clumsy.

Robin whispered to Steven, in case the dummies heard:

'Are they real men, Daddy?'

'They'd be very old if they were.'

'They could be nowadays men dressed like that.'

'I suppose so.'

'They must get very tired.'

'We must let the other children have a look.'

'I want to see if they move.'

'You can't.'

'I *want to*.'

'Do what you're told.'

'Just a few minutes, Daddy, ple—ase.'

'No.'

Steven took Robin by the ear and pulled him aside. He heard a woman behind him say loudly:

'He ought to be ashamed treating a child like that.'

Robin whimpered and then began crying.

'I can't take you anywhere without you screaming.'

'You hurt me. I never want to go out with you again.'

Robin tried to slap away his father's restraining hand. 'Give them the blessing of children, my God.' Steven started to tighten his grip on Robin's arm. Robin pulled with all his strength. He managed to wrench his arm and left Steven holding his small grey coat. Steven saw him running towards the main exit. Why couldn't he control him? He started running after him. A camel was slowly moving round a well in Ancient Egypt, an African laboured in the boiling sun to fill a large earthenware jar.

Robin had gained a considerable start. Steven cannoned into a man on the stairs and stopped to apologise. Robin had reached the top and ran on into the main hall.

When Steven found him he was turning the handle of a

164

case containing a working model of an early steam engine. The wheels moved as he went on turning. Steven grabbed his wrist roughly. He was sweating after the chase. He had hurt his leg in the collision.

'Why did you do that?' he asked in a quiet restrained voice.

Robin did not answer but went on turning, turning. Steven watched the smooth and perfect motion of the pistons. He asked again. Still the little hand went on turning the handle.

'Why?' he hissed. Robin turned his back.

In the bus Steven looked at Robin's tear-stained face. The marks were still on his cheeks. And once I needed dependants; people who would always be there, Steven thought despairingly. Now the silently reproachful child beside him was part of his life. 'To give and not to count the cost, to labour and not to seek for any reward save that of knowing that we do Thy will.' One could lavish all the love one knew and there would still be at the end the inevitable clarion call of independence and final rejection. It couldn't have been merely for this, there must be another answer, another chance.

Steven saw to his right the flags in front of the West London Air Terminal.

Sarah was standing in front of the sink in their small kitchen. Her face was flushed.

'How did he get those marks on his face?'

Steven leant against the door-frame. He said:

'I hit him.'

She stared at him apparently unable to take in this information. Steven repeated it for her: 'I hit him.'

'Do you expect a little child to respect somebody who behaves like a savage?'

'Do you expect a little child to turn his back on his father when he talks to him?'

'That depends who the father is.'

'It does, does it?'

'Yes, it does. I thought you liked him to show some spirit.'

'When was disobedience called spirit?'

'Do you expect him to be perfect at his age? You want to look at yourself before you condemn him.'

'If you mean that his disobedience stems from my being his father, I suggest you remember you're with him rather more than I am.'

'And he doesn't turn his back on me.'

'No, he knows he can spit in your face without a word of reproof.'

Sarah came towards him and said:

'Can you get out of my way? I want to go into the sitting-room.'

'No, you can stay and listen to me. I haven't finished yet.' He paused. Sarah folded her arms and looked at the floor. 'I'm not going to live my life trying to shield my children from everything that may upset them, just to please you. Minny Mouse, Freda Frog, Herbert Hare, it makes me sick. The milksop mammy song with a happy jingle. It won't harm his skin, it'll make his jerseys softer than down. My life isn't his or anybody else's. It's mine, mine.'

'Can I come through now?'

Steven stepped aside.

'You can go where the hell you like and I probably will too.'

'Go on then, if I don't have to hear you there.' She looked back and said: 'I suppose you were never young.'

When Steven came into the sitting-room, he saw Robin gently sobbing in his mother's arms. She was stroking his head and murmuring to him. Steven looked for several minutes. A stranger in my own house. Sarah's hand went on caressing. 'Mother and Child, no. 79 in your catalogues, is a delicate and moving study.' His face remained entirely impassive. At last he turned and went into the bedroom. He did not have many clothes, so it did not take long.

In the sitting-room, Sarah heard the door shut quietly.

It was four o'clock in the morning. Sarah looked at the kitchen clock again. She had listened so long at the window that she thought she had heard the clinking of money in the pockets of passers-by. It was true that he had been out for whole nights before, but he had never left like that without a word. At last she decided to go to bed. He might have got drunk and been picked up by the police. He might have hurt himself and been taken to the local hospital. She'd ask at the Police Station and the hospital when it was light.

The hospital was a low modern structure with wide lawns and contemporary concrete benches beside the well-kept paths.

She walked into the entrance marked 'Casualties'. At the desk she said:

'I wonder if you had any drunks in with cuts or anything?'

A nurse led her along a corridor into a large ward. An old man with white hair was the only person there.

'He was the only admission last night.'

'Thank you.'

Sarah was too worried to be embarrassed.

At the Police Station the constable on duty said:

'Would you like to give us a description of the missing person?'

When she got home again Robin was still asleep. He woke as she came into the bedroom.

'You didn't hear anything while I was away?'

'No, Mummy. Where's Daddy?'

'He's gone away.'

'Daddy's a horrid man.'

'Don't you dare say things like that about your father.'
Robin buried his head in his pillow.

'He's a naughty man,' mumbled Robin from the pillow.

Sarah had started to feel sick. She got up and went into the bathroom.

SEVEN

'WILL you take the next turning to the right, and then the second to the left, Mrs. Williams?' said George as Notting Hill Gate came into sight. The dual-control pedals did little to make him feel more secure. They should provide a second steering-wheel as well. Nevertheless the job had come just at the right time. A position of some responsibility, too. The Driving School he worked for could boast never having had an accident.

'Change down now,' he said.

'I was going to,' said Mrs. Williams.

'You took that one rather too fast.'

Mrs. Williams glowered. She was a large woman with several chins and an intricate network of small veins showing on her cheeks.

'When you corner take your foot right off the clutch.'

'I did.'

'I'm sorry,' said George humbly. A few unfavourable reports and he would be out of a job. 'I think you might change up to top now.' He smiled at her disarmingly. Old cow.

'Try and drive a little further out from the curb.'

'Do you want me to hit the on-coming traffic?'

'Second on the right, third on the left, please.'

'Second on the right is a one-way street.'

'Take the one after that then.'

'I should be grateful if you could say what you mean. You're paid to teach and not to confuse.'

'I'm sorry,' said an abject George.

'You're not,' said Mrs. Williams truculently.

'Change down now...'

EIGHT

DAVID saw that the door of the lodging-house was not properly closed. He pushed it open and started to climb the uncarpeted stairs. He paused on the first landing and looked round at the names on the doors. Not finding his brother's name, he climbed up to the next flight.

He rang the bell and waited. There was no answer. He tried again. They must be out. David felt relieved. Now at least he would be able to go away for a few hours to think more carefully what he would say. Before going he decided to knock. The bell might be out of order. He knocked and to his surprise the door swung open.

He walked in timidly and called his brother's name. He pushed open the sitting-room door and stood completely still. There was not a single personal possession in the room. The table-tops were bare. The carpet appeared to be newly swept. He walked through the door into the adjoining kitchen. He opened the fridge and saw that it had been cleaned out. On the top of the chest-of-drawers in the bedroom he found a child's glove, but that was all.

Suddenly he heard footsteps behind him and a voice saying:

'What do you want?'

He turned and saw a stocky man wearing a dirty white shirt with rolled-up sleeves.

'I was looking for my brother, Mr. Lifton.'

'He's gone. Just walked out one night and his wife left two days later.'

'Did either of them leave an address?'

'Not a thing. They didn't even leave a week's notice. I lose nearly fifteen pounds whenever this sort of thing happens

and with the rates going up again and most of them fiddling the meters, I can tell you I feel pretty bad about it.'
'So do I.'

In the street again he decided to try and find the local pub to see whether any more could be found out. In the gateway he tripped over a milk bottle. He picked it up and saw the note: 'Lifton, two pints.'

'The Adam and Eve' was a small pub on the next corner. From behind the bar a man shouted:
'We're not open yet.'
'I don't want a drink.'
'I'm not serving sandwiches either.'
'Did you know a Mr. Lifton?'
The barman called over to a man in the corner playing bar billiards:
'Alf, he wants to know about that Steven bloke, the one who came in evenings.'
Alf spat noisily and came over to where David was standing.
'Tell him then, you mucky bastard,' the barman said and then started laughing. Alf joined in.
'He came in last four days ago. Was it Thursday or Friday?' The barman shrugged his shoulders. 'Drank the best part of a bottle of Scotch and started swearing about his wife and kid. Asked me whether I was a family man and that sort of thing. He often did when he was drunk.'
'Didn't he have a suitcase with him that night?' asked the barman.
'Now you come to mention it, I think he did. Said he was going to catch an aeroplane or something daft like that. Said he was going to the Air Terminal the same night.'
'He didn't say where?' asked David quietly.
'He was odd'n that,' said Alf ruminatively.

'Got terrible some evenings,' added the barman.

'Never knew what he was thinking,' went on Alf.

David walked over to the door and out into the street. He felt dazed. 'My fault, my fault,' he muttered.

'Did you see the way he looked?' said the barman.

'Expect that Lifton owed him money,' said Alf, going back to his game.

David stopped when he came to a telephone box. His heart was beating hard against his rib cage. There was a tight and choking feeling at the back of his throat.

He looked up the number of Sarah's parents and dialled it. A child's voice answered.

'Can I speak to your Mummy?' David asked. It must be Robin, he thought. He heard the child go on:

'Granny's coming. Mummy isn't well.'

Soon he heard Sarah's mother: 'Who is that?'

'David Lifton. I wondered if you could . . .'

David listened to the click of the receiver being put back again.

Why did I tell that lie? Was it ever really for her or for me, he wondered. So many years ago and yet if he hadn't . . . perhaps this would never have happened. My fault, all my fault.

NINE

T H E Y were running late at the testing-centre. George looked at his watch. There ought to be at least another hour before Mrs. Williams's test was over. Several youths, awaiting their turn, were nervously pulling at cigarettes. On the waiting-room table rested a pile of well-thumbed magazines: old copies of *Vogue* and *Queen,* and *Lilliput* and *Playboy* for men. George had already looked at a couple. The usual pages were missing.

Mrs. Williams was sitting, vast and dauntless, in a corner, looking through a copy of *The Highway Code.* She looked up irritably in George's direction.

'I've already told you, there is absolutely no reason why you should stay sitting here kicking your heels about and getting on my nerves.'

George got up and walked across to the door.

'Good luck.'

She nodded to him and went on reading.

Across the road was a bus stop. George stopped for a moment's reflection. Regent's Park was only ten minutes away. On the front of the next bus to arrive he saw a notice: 'To the Zoo'.

The noise in The Monkey House was deafening and the smell offensive. But one could laugh at monkeys. They did not demand pity like the eternally restless lions and tigers or the still and solitary birds of prey. Nor did they fill one with feelings of inadequacy like the sleek gracefulness of swimming seals and sea-lions. George smiled indulgently as he watched a couple of smaller animals fighting for half a banana. Monkeys were definitely ideal temporary companions.

Further down the line of cages George saw a vast black gorilla. A small group of people were watching attentively. He moved up closer. A woman was pushing long sticks of uncooked spaghetti through a keyhole at the side of the cage. Nonchalantly the animal extended an ungrateful hand after he had consumed each offering. The next stick was momentarily withheld. George saw the creature's dark eyes roll angrily. The woman turned to George and said, smiling conspiratorially:

'He goes mad when he doesn't get what he wants.' She put her face close to the hole and said: 'Don't you, you ungrateful old beggar?'

The animal bounded across to the other side of the cage almost immediately after she had spoken and started hurling himself against the bars. He picked up handfuls of straw and hurled them impotently at the bars. Behind their protective sheet of glass the spectators laughed delightedly. George was not amused; with mild disgust he heard the woman cooing: 'Say "please", there's a good boy.'

At last the long-promised spaghetti was proffered and snatched. George could see that the animal's tormentor was going back to talk to him again. He tried to back away but found that the crowd had built up behind him. The woman was old and her hair was dyed red. Her eyes were brown and slightly protruding.

'He doesn't know who's good to him,' she said.

George felt impelled to say something now that there seemed no way of escape.

'Is he your favourite?'

'He's the most interesting. He's got such cold cruel eyes. Wicked, that's what you are,' she said, turning her face to the keyhole again.

Now that there was no more being offered, the gorilla was

sitting in a corner of his cage looking at the floor with an indifferent gaze.

'He doesn't like taking things from men. His keeper says he enjoys what I bring him more.' She paused and fixed George with her fishy eyes. 'He'll stare out any pretty woman who catches his eye.'

'He looks a bit sad at the moment,' said George.

'It's been all that taking over the years. Never had to do a thing himself. Just take, take, take, every blasted day. No wonder he looks sad, poor old beggar.'

'Well, he's got no worries now, anyway,' said George with feeling.

'You ought to be in the jungle, that's where you ought to be. He ought to be bringing in food for his children and protecting his wife. It's not natural for a great brute like that to be stuck here waited on hand and foot.'

George murmured 'Good-bye' and started to push his way through the crowd. The Monkey House had not been such a good idea. He now felt profoundly miserable. How like men are monkeys. They sit and look sad, they bound around and look sad again. They take and are afraid of taking, protecting their feelings with anger and resentment. How like a cage was the small room he now lived in and with none of the compensations enjoyed by a well-fed gorilla. He thought of the blank wall his window faced out on to and the noise of the old woman's radio next door. How could any sane men keep their heads held high with pride in the knowledge that they were self-supporting, if they lived in bed-sitting rooms?

Back to the jungle, he thought, as he pushed his way out through the turnstile.

On his arrival at the testing-centre, Mrs. Williams greeted him with her characteristic charm:

'I've been waiting for almost ten minutes and I've got people in this evening.'

'Did you pass?' asked George hopefully. Another ten lessons with her was not a thought to be cherished.

'Of course I did. The man said I was a natural driver and could have done it on half the number of lessons.'

George said:

'Perhaps we ought to be getting back if you're in a hurry.'

In the car Mrs. Williams said:

'Since you kept me waiting, I think the least you can do is to be gracious enough to allow me to drive back to my home.'

'I don't suppose I can move you.'

'I do not take kindly to such rudeness, Mr. Benson. Even fat old ladies have feelings.'

Mrs. Williams drove on in silence towards home and Hammersmith. She also drove faster than usual. George wondered what form her complaint would take and then tried to take his mind off it by calculating how much the school might charge him for the extra petrol. Why did he always have to meet domineering women? If any other man had been faced with the problems he had gone through, would he have done any better? There were things which age taught man: tolerance and humility. He looked at Mrs. Williams's tight-lipped face and sighed. Even six weeks ago he would not have suffered anybody to treat him like this. He sat back in his seat more easily as they turned into the Cromwell Road. He was no longer gritting his teeth. Humility was a really wonderful thing. He turned to Mrs. Williams and said:

'I must say, it feels as though you've been driving for years.'

'If you think you can wheedle round me like that, you're mistaken. Fat old women, like elephants, never forget.'

The smile of martyrdom was still fixed on George's face as the lorry hurtled out of the side street in front of them.

A woman on the other side of the road screamed and a man who had been looking out of his sitting-room window ran to the telephone.

When they finally lifted George into the ambulance, half a mile of motorists from Earl's Court Road to Baron's Court were cursing the Minister of Transport and wondering whether they would be having cold dinners.

At the hospital a woman was allowed to go home after three stitches and a glass of brandy.

TEN

T H E sale of Trelawn had taken place in late August and it was now mid-September.

David was looking out of the drawing-room window on to the roofs of the cars in the Fulham Road. His mother sat on the sofa behind him. She had spent most of the last month arranging the furniture they had brought from Trelawn. David thought that the small flat was far too crowded. 'We can't possibly sell that, can we, darling?'

Today Ruth looked around her with satisfaction. Really it was amazing how much one could fit into a small place with a little ingenuity. Even if Trelawn had gone for ever, they would have plenty to remember it by.

The sale and their subsequent move had been something of a blessing, David reflected. They had taken his mother's mind off other things. Nevertheless everything had got undeniably worse since he had brought back the news of Steven's disappearance. She had become more possessive and clinging, and her voice tended to become furry with emotion over the least emotional reminiscences. He had taken to going for long walks to try and get away for the odd hour. If only she would read or do something, instead of just sitting there in a dim pool of nostalgia.

At last David turned from the window and said:

'I think I'll go for a walk until tea, if that's all right.'

'Don't go now, darling, I wanted to have a talk with you.' She hesitated and then added quietly: 'You never ask me whether I'd like to come with you on your walks. I know I wouldn't be much company but you must forgive old Mumsy. The last months have been so awful. If you had asked I wouldn't have accepted. It would just have been nice, that's all.'

David heard the now familiar furry edge to her voice again. He said:

'I just thought, knowing how much you hate London and everything, that you wouldn't like to come. Besides, if I'd asked, you might have felt you had to.' David frowned. He found himself lying so often now, and the more lies told the more impossible the final undeception became. He saw his mother's smile of gratitude and lowered his eyes.

'It's ghastly to think that you'll be going away to Cambridge so soon. But still, I suppose I must be patient. After all, the term isn't so very long and when it's over it will be nearly Christmas. I've brought a few of the old decorations, so we'll have a tree.' She looked around her apprehensively. 'Of course we won't be able to have a big one like we always used to.'

Why did she have to torture herself like this? David said comfortingly:

'A small tree will be just as good, and besides,' he went on laughingly, 'we won't have so many needles to sweep up.'

'I really don't deserve a son like you, darling. In spite of everything I'm still awfully lucky.'

David avoided her eyes. Ruth looked at him lovingly, her eyes filling. He was so sweet the way compliments embarrassed him. Even when little he had been like that. She blinked to try and disperse the tears without dabbing her eyes. Really it was too terrible the way one got all weepy over anything.

'We'll have lots of parties at Christmas. All your new friends must come. I know you're going to make lots as soon as you get there. We'll roll up the carpet in here and put the furniture in my bedroom, so that there's plenty of room for dancing.' She smiled. 'You won't mind if I pop in every now and then to see how things are going?'

'I should wait till I make lots of friends before you make too many plans.'

'But I know that you're going to. There was nobody as

clever as you at Edgecombe or the grammar school. I know that was the only reason why you weren't happy. Naturally, I always secretly hoped that you would bring people home. But I know that there simply was nobody like you. You couldn't have been ashamed of your home. You weren't, were you dear?'

'Of course not. I just wasn't very good at making friends.'

How could he have asked anybody home? The only people he really knew at Edgecombe were Hotson and Chadwick and his mother wouldn't have liked any of them at the grammar school. Anyway, there had never been any time for talking to anybody there. As soon as school had been over he had had to start the long bicycle ride. They had put his reticence and early departures down to snootiness. So there had never been a hope.

'I expect you'll meet lots of girls too, dear. At your age I had any number of young gentlemen. My father used to tease me horribly about it. I'm sure it did me good though. So you mustn't mind if I tease you.' She laughed and then looked sad. David guessed that mention of girls had led her thoughts on to his eventually getting married. Some months before they left Trelawn she had talked about living in a little cottage in the village after he was married. He would, of course, live in the house and could probably get a very reasonable job in Truro or Falmouth. They need never be very far apart. Their move to London had altered Ruth's plans for the far-off future considerably. She would get a cottage in Wales and come up to London at the week-ends to see him. 'I like the country so much more, so it'll be no sacrifice for me to be there for the week-days. You must stay on here in the flat. It will help you to get properly started. Why, there'll be long walks along the Welsh cliffs, really it will be no sacrifice for me, darling.'

'In the Spring vacation we'll be able to go abroad together. I've got enough out of the sale of the house to let us go away in the summer too. You've always wanted to go to Ireland.'

'Yes, that'll be lovely.'

'But you must always remember that the last thing I want

to do is to force you to do anything with me that you don't want to do. If something more interesting crops up I'll understand. You mustn't let me become a possessive old woman.' The idea made her laugh. 'That would be simply awful, wouldn't it? When you and I go anywhere, I must feel that it's because you want to go there. Really, I'd probably be quite happy all alone in Wales.'

David said nothing for a moment but the look of pain and anxiety on his mother's face made him say:

'I want to go abroad. I've never been and have always wanted to travel.'

Ruth got up, smiling. She said:

'We're going to have such fun. It all makes me feel so much younger. But now there's masses still to do to get this place in order. I haven't even lined the drawers in my bedroom with paper.' She turned in the doorway. 'We'll be having tea soon.'

As soon as she had left the room, David went over to the sofa. Beside where his mother had been sitting was a pile of letters. The top one was addressed to a house agent in Tenby.

In her bedroom Ruth hummed gently to herself as she picked single sheets of newspaper and folded them into the shapes of the drawers. Occasionally a story would catch her eye and she stopped to read. A divorce, a fraud, a story about a woman who had had a successful eye operation, all gained her brief attention.

She had reached the last drawer when she saw it. Just one paragraph near the bottom of the back page of an evening paper. At first she thought she was going to faint. In spite of her trembling she managed to sit down on the edge of the bed without falling before she got there. Blindly she repeated the word: 'Critical, critical, critical.' The date at the top of the page showed that it had happened a month ago.

At half past five David put down the book he had been reading and got up. Hadn't she said something about tea?

He knocked on Ruth's bedroom door and entered. She was sitting at the dressing-table mirror making up carefully. David coughed cautiously. When she turned to face him, he could see that she was nervous and excited. She was fidgeting uneasily with a small eyelash brush.

'I've just remembered, I've got an invitation to dinner this evening. Silly of me to have forgotten.' She paused. Visiting-time would be over by seven-thirty. That would mean she'd be back by eight o'clock. 'I must be going crazy in my old age, dear. It was a cocktail party, so I'll be back in time to cook you supper.'

'You're getting that stuff on your hands, Mummy,' David looked at her anxiously. In recent weeks she had hardly spent any time in front of a mirror.

'So I am, darling. You see I only just remembered in time and have been in an awful rush. I'm quite stupid when I'm in a rush.'

'Who's giving the party?'

'Oh, an old girl friend I haven't seen for years. Not since before the war.'

'I see,' said David doubtfully.

'Perhaps you could get me a taxi, dear? Otherwise I'm going to be late.'

Obediently David turned.

When she heard the front door shut, she jumped up from her stool and dragged a chair over to the wardrobe. She pulled down half a dozen hat boxes and carefully selected a simple black hat. Next she opened a drawer and picked out her jewel case. She chose a brooch consisting of a single large diamond surrounded with pearls. It would look stark and austere on her black coat. She went over to the dressing-table and glanced at the result in the mirror. It would do very nicely.

In the sitting-room she poured herself a large gin. She was beginning to feel stronger when she heard David's footsteps in the hall. Quickly she ran into the kitchen and emptied the bowl of fruit on the table into a paper bag.

❧

'A visitor, Mr. Benson, a visitor ... a visitor ... a visitor.' George heard the words dimly echoing. Slowly he crawled out of the vacuum of his anaesthetised isolation. 'Come on now, Mr. Benson, wake up. You've never had a visitor before.'

Ruth saw his eyelids flutter and heard his breathing change. The nurse turned to her and said:

'He isn't used to talking, so you mustn't tire him.'

❧

George still had a bandage round his head. One of his feet was raised and held up by several weights on a pulley. The bedclothes were humped up on a square frame over the lower part of his body. How utterly helpless he looked. Ruth came cautiously closer. She felt a warm rising feeling of love and pity under her diaphragm.

'George, George,' she whispered.

He opened his eyes again and shut them. When he re-opened them he was surprised still to see somebody remarkably like Ruth standing beside his bed. Probably those drugs. He was about to call out for the nurse when the vision spoke again.

'Can you recognise me, George? It's Ruth.'

George moved his head from side to side. Ruth stared at him in terror. Perhaps they hadn't been telling the truth when they had told her on the telephone that the accident had not affected his mind. She said louder:

'It's Ruth, who you used to live with. Ruth, you must remember Ruth?'

George saw from the corner of his eye that the man in the next bed had raised himself on to an elbow so that he could hear better. He was now in no doubt.

'George darling, I read about it in the papers and came at once. I hope you're not cross with me for not warning you.'

George strove to try and decide whether she was being sarcastic. What possible reason could she have come for, after everything that had happened, if it was not to mock him in his infirmity? If she had read it in the papers, why hadn't she come earlier? Ruth watched his expression of bewilderment and no longer felt frightened. It was the same expression she had seen whenever he made a mistake with his needlework or didn't know what answer to give to Steven.

'You look so silly with your feet up in the air like that, darling.' She was leaning forward towards him and smiling, smiling.

'I expect so,' he said defensively.

'Don't get all cross, you old bear. Because I'm not going to be cross with you.'

'Good. I'm not feeling well enough for a row.'

'I meant that, George. I want to forget everything ... if ... if you're not living with somebody else. You're not, are you ... say you're not.'

Her voice had risen to an imploring wail. George sensed the eyes of everybody else in the ward on them. The man immediately to his right was muttering: 'Disgusting, disgusting.'

'No, I'm not,' he hastily agreed.

'I'm so, so happy, darling. Then we really can begin again?'

George nodded his agreement. He was filled with a profound feeling of well-being, it caressed his shattered body with fingers softer than peach skin.

'I'm happy too,' he said at last. But what if this was merely a passing mood of sentimentalism fostered by pity? Her re-

184

jection when he had rung her up those months ago had been as real as this strange reversal.

'Are you sure about what you're doing?'

'Yes, as sure as I ever am about anything, but you know how hopeless I am.'

'But weren't you equally sure about never seeing me again after I left?'

'I know that you were foolish once but now time has healed. I'm not strong enough or silly enough to keep away from you for the sake of my pride. I only realised how much I needed you when I read about your accident. And besides I just *know* that some things can't be undone whatever happens afterwards. Now I can look back more clearly without anger. I was only blinded for a little while. I must have known it for a long time, known I mean that I wanted you back because I had forgiven. It was only the article that told me, that forced me, to have the courage to discover whether you would ever come back.'

'There are things which have to be felt rather than thought. I know that,' said George hoping that this was the right answer.

Ruth nodded. George was afraid for a moment that she was going to cry. But she blinked away her tears and said:

'I don't think I've ever really felt so like crying with happiness. I thought it was all a lie, but now I know it's true.'

She dabbed her eyes with a small handkerchief and sat looking at him, smiling through her tears.

It was only then that she was aware of the bag of fruit that she had been clasping all the time.

'I've brought you these. I don't expect they're all that good. But I'll bring back more every day and much nicer. Lots of grapes and pears.'

Suddenly George was laughing. It was all so intolerably funny. He remembered the woman at the zoo and the gorilla and then about his present situation. Then he thought of something else.

'Do you remember when you used to bring me fruit twenty years ago?'

'And in hospital too. How could I ever forget the days that changed my life?'

David was sitting listening to a concert when Ruth got back to the flat. She hadn't waited for the lift, but had run up the stairs.

'David, darling,' she gasped. 'He's coming back. George is coming back ... I can hardly believe it, but it's true.'

She ran across the room lightly and flopped into a chair. Beethoven thundered on unheard. David's mouth hung open, slowly the corners turned upwards into a smile.

'Everything is going to be all right after all,' he said quietly. He repeated the words several times to convince himself. Then quite suddenly he leapt to his feet and, running over to the radio, turned it up as high as it would go and, with generous sweeping movements, started to conduct.

ELEVEN

GEORGE had been out of hospital a week already and Ruth felt that he was ready for the journey. Of course they would stop off on the way at hotels, so that he did not get overtired.

The car was loaded by 9.00 a.m. so they would get a nice early start.

Carefully Ruth lifted George's feet up into the car. The marvellous thing about it all was that he did not mind being helped. She had been awfully worried in case he had tried to do everything himself. But George was so sensible over everything.

The cottage in Wales had been kept a careful secret. So had the sale of Trelawn. He might blame himself or get angry unless it was made impossible for him. But how could he possibly be annoyed if they were already on their way for the first holiday together since their reunion? Ruth smiled at her ingenuity.

Nearly an hour later George was looking down at the water under Staines Bridge as they drove on west. Funny to think that a month ago he had been certain that he would never be making the journey to Trelawn again. But life was like that. It just happens, just a lot of chances. An attack of earache, a bottle of scent, a careless lorry driver and a pile of old newspapers. Perhaps it was the unexpectedness of everything that made it all worth while.

As the suburbs gave way to the fields he glanced at Ruth's hands on the wheel, holding it with the strength of the past. She still wore the rings he had seen when he first met her. Today she seemed so strong and resolute, so dependable in her large fur coat. Her face wore an expression of quiet thoughtfulness.

'What are you thinking of?' he asked.

'Oh, nothing dear. Only how we used to play games with the children on this road. A penny for every cow, two for a goat ... you remember?'

'I remember.'

And George also remembered Steven. A momentary feeling of disquiet led him to ask:

'What happened to Steven?'

'He went away.'

'I see. I'm sorry.'

Ruth nodded. Poor Steven, thought George, what chance had he got against the unpredictability of lorry drivers and newspapers in drawers?

He looked at Ruth and was surprised to see that she was smiling.

'Nothing else has changed, darling, has it?'

'Nothing really,' said George, looking down at his legs.

'Promise you'll never ever try to run away again?'

George thought of the wheelchair in the back of the car.

'I promise.'

'Even if I take you to live in a tiny doll's house without much money?'

'Yes, yes,' said George, laughing. He had forgotten how funny Ruth could be.